Murder on

By

Christopher Mills

Murder On Safari

This book is a work of fiction

and except in the cases

where historical fact

or actual place names are used,

any resemblance to actual persons,

living or dead

is purely coincidental.

About this story and the author

I have been involved in the business of performing Murder Mystery evenings and weekends for the past twenty five years with my company Murder by Design. During that time I have written and produced over forty plots which myself and my team of actors have presented in over 800 performances to an estimated 50,000 guests.

One of my very first plots was 'Murder on Safari' and this book is based around the plotline which the actors use to create their interpretation of the character they are portraying at that performance. This is a working plot and so there is a very strong chance that the story you are about to read is being enacted by me and my team somewhere in the country for real.

Of course we don't actually kill anyone. That never goes down well with guests, particularly over dinner and even more so if they have paid for the privilege.

But you know what I mean.....

I created and have always played the part of PC Bailey and I have great pleasure in handing him over to you to read the backstory of my favourite bumbling copper.

I hope that you enjoy discovering the plot and just 'whodunnit' as much as I have enjoyed writing it and as much as our guests have enjoyed and continue to enjoy seeing the plot revealed over the course of an evening, usually over a wonderful dinner and some fine wine.

Christopher Mills

July 2014

To my wonderful family and my friends

who have had to put up with me going on

about this first book forever!

And especially to John Butler for his inspiration

Curves and Edges...

The PC Bailey Series

Murder on Safari

Who killed Santa Claus?

The Mucklington Murders

Chapter One

They are never going to believe this back at the station, thought PC Bailey as he stood in the hallway of the grandest house he had ever seen in his life. Exeter Cathedral itself isn't any better than this, from what he remembered when he had visited it on a school trip as a small boy, and yet this is just someone's house! I hate to think how they do the high dusting in here, he mused.

'So, you're Police Constable Bailey I presume?' boomed a voice next to him that brought him sharply back to reality.

He turned to see a woman of indeterminate age. In fact, on second glance he wasn't even sure it was a woman but he thought it would be safer to stick with his initial impression.

'Yes Madam I am PC Bailey and may I say well done for knowing that the PC stands for 'Police Constable'? A lot of people make the mistake of thinking that PC must be my initials which is wrong as my name is John which would be J Bailey or PCJ Bailey but that could confuse people don't you think er Madam? And whom might I have the pleasure of addressing?'

'Well you're late to start with, you also have the appearance of someone who has been drawn through a hedge backwards and has had a very close encounter with a good deal of hay. On top of that you seem to be gabbling, I don't approve of anyone gabbling, it is difficult enough to understand people who lack the education to speak proper English and choose to speak in the dialect of their local area, as you choose to do, without the added obstacle of gabbling as well. I am of course fluent in over twenty languages and literally hundreds of local dialects. So all in all not a very auspicious start is it Bailey? On top of all of that when the person who has organised the entire expedition, and who has appeared in numerous newspaper articles and whose name has appeared on the front cover of at least two dozen highly acclaimed books on the perils of the African continent, whose voice has been heard on countless programmes on the BBC home service and, if my observation is correct, is the only person in the room sporting a signature pith helmet and full safari outfit and yet you as the Policeman, the 'eyes and ears' of the Law of this fair land we lovingly call England, has completely failed to recognise me as the one and only, Lady Agatha Plantagenet, the world-famous explorer'?

'Ah yes, I see that Madam. In fact now that you come to mention it and I see the hat and..'

'As I said, it is a Pith helmet, dear boy, a Pith helmet do you understand? It is not just a hat' Lady Agatha interjected. 'It's part of my signature; I am never without this marvellous headwear. The pith helmet originated as something worn by people of European origin when they visited the tropics. The hat was commonly made from the pith of the Indian Swamp Plant Aeschynomene aspera and designed to shade the wearer's head and face from the sun. There were a number of designs but I favour the Wolseley pattern, adopted by our boys in the services, and offering far more protection from the sun with its swept back brim design, than the earlier Foreign Services Issue afforded.'

'Yes thank you Madam, very educational' Bailey thought for a moment and then added. 'Don't these sorts of helmet usually have feathers or something sticking out of the top?'

Lady Agatha was by now into full lecturing mode and was going to let Bailey know the error of his latest comment with another torrent of information.

'My dear man, you clearly have little experience of this sort of thing. I can tell that foreign travel and all things Colonial are beyond you. I expect this whole trip here from wherever you have come from is probably the furthest that you have travelled away from your place of birth in a single day?'

Bailey thought for a moment but before he could comment that he had on one occasion taken a trip to Blackpool which had been much further, but then he thought this probably wouldn't stand up as a good example of his ability to travel as he had, in fact, got lost during two changes at Bristol and Birmingham and ended up for a time travelling towards Crewe. He chose to just nod and leave it at that.

'I thought as much. Well feathers were worn by Governors and Governors-General. They wore ten inch red and white swan feathers. Army personnel prefer the khaki version of course and often add a cap badge while our Navy Officers like the plain white hat with just a little blue edging to the top of the puggarree.'

'Of course, Pith Helmet' Bailey continued, 'it becomes fairly obvious then that you are indeed who you say you are.'

'Then perhaps all of your powers of deduction are not lost. This evening should be fairly simple to follow, even for you Bailey, so there shouldn't be any problems.'

Bailey slowly absorbed the words that Lady Agatha spoke and linked them with the information that he had already been given by his Sergeant before leaving on the twelve minutes past four train from Exeter St David's station.

His gentle, loving wife Sarah had accompanied him to the platform and brought along their three children William, Edwin and Kathleen to see him off. It had been quite an occasion but then John Bailey didn't get many opportunities like this and he was very proud that he had been selected.

'Now don't worry yourself my love, me and the children will be perfectly fine. My mother is popping over later and staying for dinner so I won't really have time to miss you!'

PC Bailey looked crestfallen for a moment but then he looked into his Sarah's twinkling green eyes. The eyes that from the first time he saw them, he knew he would be in love with this woman forever and knew that she was just pulling his leg.

Smiling, he bent down and embraced his children for one last hug and then took his wife in his arms and lifted her bodily off the ground and twirled her slowly as he kissed her cheek. Sarah theatrically pounded on his arms to release her while the children jumped around shrieking at this spectacle before them.

He placed her back on the ground and in one motion picked up his case and bag and stepped backwards and upwards into the carriage. Then, making sure not to collect any people in the swinging action of the door, he closed the door and promptly reappeared through the open carriage door window.

'All 'board!' came the cry from the guard just as the minute hand on the large station clock swung to 12 minutes past the hour. His shrill whistle made the signal to the driver and all at once steam and smoke bellowed out from the engine engulfing the people on the platform completely for a few seconds.

'I'll be back by lunchtime tomorrow, I should think, on the nine-thirty-six from Bristol Temple Meads. Now children, be very good for your mother. I love you all' His words trailed off as the driver transferred the power of the engine to the huge wheels and with a jolt the train began to move forwards.

Sarah gathered up their young daughter Kathleen in her arms and walked along the platform keeping up with the train as it picked up speed.

'Take care John, I love you and I'll see you tomorrow.'

PC Bailey waved back blowing kisses as Sarah and Kathleen stopped competing with the increasing speed and waved wildly, the boys continued to run alongside for as long as they could but eventually even they had to give up.

'Look after the girls' he shouted back as the boys stood at the end of the platform, out of breath but smiling and waving wildly in the direction of their father, who was already disappearing from view. In a short while the train was clear of the station and after the 'chuff-chuff-chuff' could no longer be heard, only the long trail of smoke rising up into the Summer sky was soon the only evidence the train had ever been there at all.

He stood for another few minutes waving from the window until the train turned slowly to the right and the station buildings gave way firstly to a few commercial properties, a garage, a timber yard and then the back gardens of houses which backed on to the railway embankment. Whenever he passed this way out of Exeter St David's, he always had the same thought about these houses and how the gardens had high walls on each side which provided such private spaces from their immediate neighbours and yet hundreds of people peered into them, if only for a few seconds, every day which probably made them the most overlooked 'private' gardens in the city. He pulled on the leather strap in the door and the glass began to rise, finally snapping into the closed position. In an instant the environment inside the narrow corridor changed as the noise and smells coming in from the open window were replaced with the sounds of the creaking of the carriage and the rhythm of the wheels as it passed over the rails.

Bailey turned from the window and opened the sliding compartment door and crossed to his window seat. He had arrived early enough to secure a good seat facing the engine. He had not had a great deal of experience of train travel but what he had, had taught him that, for him at least, he much preferred to be looking at where he was going rather than where he had been. As it turned out he had his pick in any case as although the train had looked fairly busy with the number of people getting on at Exeter, he found himself sharing his compartment of six seats with only one other person, a man perhaps in his mid-fifties with a small grey beard and dressed fully in tweeds and plus fours. As Bailey took his seat he noticed the man was already engrossed in a copy of The Times and as he drew on his pipe the man was clearly working on the crossword page.

'Ah I see you are doing the crossword then' said Bailey.

The man looked up with a start and for a moment appeared irritated at this interruption. On realising that he was being addressed by a

Policeman, he visibly softened his approach and merely said' Am I doing something wrong Officer?'

'No, no of course not, I was just noticing that you are doing the crossword.'

'Well done' said the man returning to his paper.

'I quite like doing them myself. I always think how clever it is that if you get the right answer it fits with one of the other clues going the other way.'

The man lowered his paper and looked back at Bailey with an expression of bewilderment, but before he could utter a sound Bailey continued,

'And if you're really lucky, that word can sometimes give you a clue as to what the other word is, amazing isn't it?' At this, he turned to look out of the window at the landscape as it rapidly whisked by, occasionally blocked out by the smoke from the engine as it swirled along the length of the train.

The man continued to look in Bailey's direction for some moments before finally giving up trying to fathom the same question that had been asked by many and never fully answered by anyone….'How had this man made it into the Police force?' He returned once again to the task in hand, a particularly tricky cryptic clue; a problem altogether far simpler.

Bailey continued to ponder the wonder of crosswords for a while before his thoughts returned to the reason why he was here in the first place and the voice of his Sergeant from their meeting this morning at eighty thirty, rang clear in his mind, 'Now Bailey, although we would always be able to argue that the only reason you have been given this duty is because Inspector Lansdowne cannot attend himself and the local constabulary from Stonefield are playing skittles in the South West finals in Bideford which, in their opinion, is far more important than a bit of crowd control for a bunch of toffs going off on a long holiday. It still doesn't mean that there needs to be any mistakes. So think carefully, think twice….no make that three times, about any actions you might want to take before you take them, always be near a telephone so that you can ask someone, anyone, if you need to make any decision other than which sandwich to eat next, don't lose any of the guests and generally and above all else just don't muck it up alright?'

Sound advice thought Bailey. With a Sergeant like that, holding him in such high regard it was really no wonder at all why he had been picked for this job. After all on experience alone he was the obvious choice wasn't he? Fifteen years in the force and not a sniff of promotion. That took real determination he thought. His father, Albert (nicknamed 'Old Bailey') had managed twenty-five years with no promotion and had his Sergeant not commented on more than one occasion that he was pretty confident he would be able to beat that record?

There was the sound of the door to the carriage sliding open and Bailey looked up to see a young man in the uniform of a Great Western Railway Ticket Collector, stood in the doorway. 'Tickets please gentleman, may I have your tickets?'

'You're the ticket collector' said Bailey.

'Oh God' sighed the man from behind his paper.

Bailey produced his railway pass ticket from his top pocket and handed it to the collector who quickly scrutinised it before punching the ticket with a small rectangular hole with a wavy side on one end of it.

'I am indeed' remarked the man handing the ticket back. 'Oh yes, I'm sure there isn't much that gets past you Constable'

'I would think an entire brass band playing a Souza march could go past and this copper wouldn't even notice' thought the man to himself. However, he said nothing and just grimaced at the collector as he handed his ticket over.

The rest of the journey passed without much incident apart from the moment when they entered the first tunnel.

'I say' said Bailey, leaning over to the man still trying to immerse himself in his newspaper and trying desperately to avoid the gaze of the Policeman.

'I say, isn't it amazing?'

'What is?' replied the man nervously.

'Well surely you have noticed. We are in a tunnel and yet I can still see you!'

'Yes I had noticed that we are in a tunnel but that isn't really very unusual on this particular journey. In fact we pass through more than one such tunnel. I take it that you haven't made this journey very often, if at all?'

'It's true to say that I don't get out much' replied Bailey, 'but it has only just occurred to me that somehow they must know when to turn on the lights because here we are in the tunnel and yet I can still see you. I think that's really clever don't you?'

The man sat dumbstruck. On the one hand it was true that he had never given it much thought but clearly the lights remained on in the carriage all of the time, they were not operated by either the driver or the guard when they approached tunnels, wasn't that obvious to everyone?

However, on the other hand perhaps it was this sort of simplistic observation of everyday occurrences which made good Policeman and that perhaps he was underestimating this public servant opposite him. He pondered this thought for a couple of seconds while looking at the smiling face of PC Bailey who sat awaiting his reply. No he thought to himself, it's not that he is observationally astute, he's just useless. However, he actually replied.

'You may have a point there Constable it is not really something I had considered. I guess it's just part of the good service that we get from the trains these days!'

With that he lifted his newspaper a little higher and hoped that this journey would be over quickly. In fact he even thought about getting off the train and catching the next one but no matter how much this Policeman annoyed him; he would grin and bear it because he couldn't miss his connection. Otherwise he would arrive late for his evening out with a very lovely woman who he was meeting later on. Her Christian name, she once told him, was originally Swedish and he smiled at how much pleasure she brought into his life and she in turn had told him on more than one occasion that he did the same for her. He was really looking forward to meeting her as their time together was precious and never long enough. They had become much more than friends and although her life was very complicated, he hoped that one day fairly soon she would be his for good. In the meantime, he would wait it out and enjoy the time they spent together.

As the train slowed over the points just outside Midloxton station, Bailey was already up and out of his seat and taking down his suitcase from the overhead luggage shelf.

Bailey noticed that the man remained seated as he pulled open the door that led into the corridor.

'I take it this isn't your stop then Sir?' Bailey enquired slightly distracted as he wrestled his case through the door which was proving difficult. This was because as the train slowed on its approach to the platform it caused the sliding door to close for the umpteenth time onto his case.

'No indeed Constable, I am travelling on further to Bristol'

'Ah, well best you don't get off here then, good day'

'Yes, thank you, good day' said the man returning to his paper with a sigh of relief that he would be alone for the rest of the journey and his own private thoughts of what he was sure would be a memorable evening ahead.

With a hiss and a huge cloud of steam the train came to a stop and immediately doors were opening along the length of the train and people began to alight onto the platform. 'Midloxton!' shouted the guard. Even though this was a fairly sleepy, out of the way village, the station itself was an important change point for those who wished to travel on the West Coast branch line serving such places as Porlock Weir and Minehead. For this reason, there were always a good number of people changing trains at this stop.

Bailey stepped down on to the platform and was promptly met by an officious looking man with a large grey handlebar moustache and blue eyes which were just visible under the stiff peak of his cap, who saluted him which, given that he was carrying a number of different coloured flags in his hand was no mean feat, and said 'I take it Sir from the number on your collar that you are Police Constable Bailey; my name is Johnson. I am the Under Station Master here at Midloxton Halt. I received a communication from our Exeter office in accordance with Great Western Railway Rule 217a which clearly states that "Great Western Railway staff may be employed from time to time to provide assistance to members of His Majesty's Police Force in the execution of their official duties". This communication stated that I was to look out for you and to provide you with transport to Motley Hall where I am led to believe the guests who are in your charge are already assembling.'

'Oh well that's very nice of you and there really is no need to salute me you know.'

'Thank you Sir' said Johnson saluting again.

'Transport you say, I didn't expect a car or anything. I thought it would just be a taxi.'

'Ah yes, well Constable there's a problem.'

'A problem?'

'Yes' continued Johnson stuttering a little. 'You see there was a car to pick you up, but Midloxton isn't the biggest police station in the country and so from time to time PC Meadowford, the village constable, often does errands around the place if he gets a loan of the car from the main station in Stonefield'.

'What sort of errands?' asked Bailey with genuine interest.

'Well, it can vary. Sometimes it might be as simple as giving Mrs Shaw from Pond End Farm, a lift into town to the chemist or to see Dr Bracing. But sometimes, it might be a bit more complicated or urgent, such as last month when he had to rush Ivy Stamford to the cottage hospital because she was having a baby. Unfortunately, the road had more bumps in it than

Ivy's condition could stand and the baby was delivered in the back of the Police car just outside the Golden Stumps Inn. It was a wonderful moment when he opened the door and lifted up the tiny infant wrapped in his cloak. Ivy was so pleased with the service; guess what she decided to name the little lad?'

'Er Stumpy? no wait maybe Golden?' volunteered Bailey with a hopeful look on his face.

'No. Bobby of course!' exclaimed Johnson with a slight look of annoyance.

'Anyway, as I say, PC Meadowford had the car ready for you today so that he could whisk you up to the Hall as soon as you arrived but unfortunately Albert Dartmouth, the funeral director had a bit of an emergency. It appears that his second hearse wouldn't start this morning which meant that the less important family mourners of Walter Elscott, would miss their father's funeral. Mr Elscott was a formidable force in the local community, not only because he owned most of the farmland hereabouts but also because he had only recently finished raising funds for the local church bells which will, rather ironically, ring for the very first time at his funeral. It was the final effort of pulling on the rope to get the bells installed, which he personally chose to do, that caused him to have the heart attack that killed him. Funny how these things turn out isn't it? Anyway the upshot is that the car designated for you has been otherwise diverted to help out in this local emergency which means we will have to rely on plan B, which is this sack truck.'

'Oh well that's very decent of you, but really you needn't have gone to so much trouble. I mean you are probably kept busy with all these trains and suchlike.'

'Oh no, you misunderstand' said Johnson raising his hands in front of him as if to halt the conversation from going any further. 'I am only lending you the sack truck. I can't leave the station. I am an employee of the Great Western Railway Company and must remain on or around it's premises for the duration (notwithstanding tea breaks and twenty minutes luncheon break which can be taken at any time between eleven forty five and one forty five but may not be used for deduction from the working day should the employee choose to waiver the aforementioned breaks). It's all there in the GWR Regulations Handbook for employees paragraphs fourteen through to nineteen and fifty one to fifty seven A (subsection four). You will still have to push the bags to Motley Hall yourself; I just thought it might make it a bit easier'.

'I see. Well I am sure I will manage. Thank you for the kind loan of the truck'.

Bailey had been informed by his Sergeant that he would be staying over at Motley Hall and would be returning to Exeter the next morning after the party had left to meet their ship. He had therefore packed himself, with Sarah's assistance, a case and an overnight bag as well as a packet of sandwiches for the journey. He hoped he had thought of everything.

Johnson spent a few minutes expertly loading Bailey's bags onto the sack truck and then with a final tug of the leather straps he expertly wheeled the truck to the station entrance; he pointed to the road to the right. 'Just follow this road for about a mile and a half, give or take. You will go through the village and then arrive at the 'witches' hat' crossroads. You can't miss it really; in front of you will be an old thatched cottage which has a crooked roof which makes it look like a giant hat, the sort that you might find on a witch in the storybooks. Of course, there are no real witches but that's where the name of the crossroads comes from. Anyway, from there you take a left and walk on another half mile or so and then the entrance to the Hall will come up on your left. Go past the gatehouse, under the arch, up the driveway and when it forks, you should stay to the right because as you have your cases with you I would assume that you would want to drop them off at the servants entrance before you make your way around to the front of the Hall and arrive properly so to speak.'

'Oh yes, very proper, good thought Mr Johnson. I will do exactly as you suggest. There doesn't look like there will be a change in the weather but all the same I had better get a step on as I am now going to be cutting it very fine to get there on time and first impressions are the ones that count first aren't they?'

Johnson nodded in agreement. 'The weather has been dry all day but there is a storm expected later coming in from the West. The men have been working all day in the fields getting in the hay.'

With that Bailey set out along the road pushing his bags ahead of him. It soon became clear that although the sack truck appeared a good idea and apparently in good condition, the fact remained that for some inexplicable reason the wheels seemed to snag as soon as he made the slightest deviation from straight ahead. He hoped that GWR paid more attention to their trains than they did to their sack trucks. At one point he considered leaving the truck behind but on balance decided that it was still probably better to persevere and Johnson had gone to a lot of trouble.

Had Bailey not been quite so concerned with the control of the truck he might have noticed the funeral car drawing silently up at the station behind him and he might have seen how Johnson had animatedly signalled the car to quickly reverse around the corner of the station house out of view. He might also have noticed the slightest twitch of the curtain behind the dirty window of the tired old cottage that gave its name to the crossroads on the far side of the village. If he had looked very hard he might even have noticed the figure that stood motionless behind that curtain and watched him as he struggled along with the defective hand transport that he had been given by the Under Station Master.

But instead, it appeared that Bailey saw none of this and his journey passed uneventfully right up until the moment a driverless hay cart came careering around the bend of the road heading straight for him causing him to abandon his belongings and dive headlong into the brambles. The cart collided with the sack truck causing the cart to jolt violently upwards and sideward and in doing so showered the hapless Bailey in hay as he lay there in the brambles.

For a while he lay there in a daze but the pain from the tiny thorns cutting into his legs and his back and just about everywhere else brought him back to his senses. He discovered that he was in fact suspended in mid-air in a very large bramble bush that had completely grown over a small brook that he could hear gurgling not far beneath him. He moved his arms but realised that he was well and truly stuck and that any vigorous efforts to extricate himself resulted in a good deal of pain and the possibility that he would dislodge himself from his thorny bed and be deposited in the water below. He had no idea how deep that water might be so this was becoming a serious problem. As he lay there wondering how exactly he was going to ever get free he heard the sound of a motor car coming along the road which stopped very close to him. He heard someone alight from the vehicle and then a voice.

'Are you all right Constable, you seem to be in somewhat of a jam?' said a woman in an accent that Bailey didn't recognise. But then he had never heard an American from the Deep South before. Bailey just thought she was foreign.

'Yes Madam. I find that I am rather stuck. I had to jump out of the way of a hay cart' replied Bailey

'Well don't worry. I'm sure I have some rope in the car. I'll go and get it and then we can pull you upright and ya'll be out of there in no time' said the woman.

'Right ho Madam! I'll just stay here then while I'm waiting if that's all right?

The woman moved off and he could hear the sounds of her rummaging around as he lay there looking up at the sky. He noticed the clear blue sky was now beginning to be joined by wisps of white cloud, the start of a change in the weather he thought to himself. The woman returned.

'Right, now here is the end of the rope. I think I can probably feed it straight into your hand, yes success! Now hold on one moment while I tie it to the car and then you can pull yourself upright.

Bailey felt the rope in his hand and awaited the signal from his unknown rescuer.

'Good now take a firm hold and pull slowly on the rope' said the woman.

Bailey did as he was told and as he took up the slack in the rope he felt his body sink further into the brambles but then just as he thought he would end up in the brook, he felt his feet connect with the edge of the embankment and with further effort he tipped forwards and found himself upright once again. With a few swift, yet painful movements of his limbs he freed himself from the brambles and walked towards the woman who stood in the road next to her bright red sports car.

'My name is Mary-Belle Devine. I was on my way up to Motley Hall to join the safari party when I saw the horse and cart. I couldn't see the driver so that was who I was looking out for when I saw you lying here in the bushes. I take it you weren't driving the cart yourself were you?

'No madam I wasn't; I was also making my way up to Motley Hall with my cases on that sack truck that you now see spread out across the road. When I turned the bend and that cart came straight for me, I had to leap in the bushes or that would have been the end of me! My name is PC Bailey by the way. That is PC meaning Police Constable of course rather than my initial which is J because my name is John. I must thank you for helping me out of the, the, well my situation.'

'Oh it was no problem. I could hardly leave you there, a Policeman and all.'

Bailey brushed himself down, carefully removing some of the thorny branches that were still attached to his uniform. He walked back down the road towards the cart which had skidded off on to the verge but had mercifully remained upright and the horse now stood quietly between the shafts but still breathing heavily. Mary-Belle moved around the cart and inspected the horse's front legs. She placed her hand just above the hoof and gently lifted the leg. The horse at first made to start but she calmed the beast instantly. After a moment she let the leg down again and did the same procedure with the other legs. The horse offered no further resistance.

'Hmm, well I'm no expert, but nothing appears to be broken so that's good' she said.

'Well Miss Devine, you say you are no expert, but you have a remarkable way with that horse. Look at how calm he is now.'

'I have twenty-five horses on my own ranch and I have been around horses since I was a little girl. I still wouldn't say that I am any sort of expert but I guess I have a knack. You just need to show them confidence and then they trust you. One thing I would say though is that I think your knowledge of horses is probably less than mine as this 'he' is in fact a lady.' A broad smile broke out on her face as she said it and Bailey found himself caught off guard by just how strikingly good looking this young woman was.

'Yes right. Good, well, fine thing really. I like your car by the way, it looks very new' he gabbled trying to look as if he hadn't been affected by her smile.

'Why thank you. I picked it up only yesterday. It's a Mercedes Benz 500K roadster, I am glad you like it. Unfortunately, as you can see I don't have any room in the passenger seat or the trunk but I can always carry on up to the Hall which should be just up around the next corner if my directions are correct and then I can drop my things and come back for you?'

'Oh no, no need for that' said Bailey. 'I'll just pack up my bags back on the truck and then I'll make my own way. Your directions do indeed appear to match the ones I received from Mr Johnson at the station so I shall be there in no time at all. What shall we do with the horse and cart though?'

Mary-Belle looked around her 'Hmm that's a very good point. There is a gateway over there let's see if we can move it into that field and then we can send back some help from the Hall to sort things out. It must belong to someone after all and you would imagine they are going to miss it very soon unless something has happened to them of course.'

She expertly manoeuvred the horse around and through the gate while Bailey held it as wide open as he could. The gate had seen much better days and it flopped around causing him to need to hold it with both hands and to wrap one leg around the upright to steady it. It was just as she was walking around the cart that she suddenly stopped and bent forward near the hind quarters of the horse. She brushed her hand softly across the skin causing the now placid horse to flinch and flick her head. 'There is something here I think you should see Constable'.

Bailey having closed the gate once more with some effort discovered that the leg of his uniform was now covered in yellow and green streaks from the lichen that was growing on the gate. He attempted to brush it off, without much effect, as he came over and made a closer inspection of the spot she was pointing at. He followed her finger to a small tuft of brown hair that was sticking out. At first he thought it was just part of the horse.

Mary-Belle carefully rubbed the area directly around the object and then deftly pulled it out without the horse making a single movement. 'That is a dart PC Bailey. This horse did not bolt of its own accord. The question is why someone would want it to do that. Why would somebody want this horse to bolt with the result that if you had not been so quick thinking you could have been very seriously injured or even killed!?'

Bailey thought for a moment. 'Well it's an interesting question. Someone could have seen that I was walking up the road but if that were the case, then why would anyone want to harm me. Who even knows that I am here apart from the Under Station Master and he was kind enough to lend me his sack truck. That doesn't sound like the action of someone who wanted to cause me harm now does it? We must also look at the possibility that someone, perhaps a young child was playing with a catapult perhaps and hit the horse by mistake, which sent the poor beast running down the road. If that was the case, then it was nothing more than a coincidence that I was coming along the road at the same point in time.'

Mary-Belle looked as if she wanted to say more but instead kept her own counsel. 'Now PC Bailey, if you would be so good as to help me here. We must get this horse out of these shafts and then we can tie her reins to that tree. She will be quite safe until we can get some help. I can't understand why the owner hasn't turned up yet. Somebody must me missing this rig?'

In a short while the horse was free from the cart and appeared to be no worse the wear for its earlier ordeal and quietly grazed while the policeman and Mary-Belle made their way back to the gate.

He carefully opened the gate once more trying to avoid further damage to his uniform and they left the field.

'Thank you Bailey. Now are you sure that you are going to be all right? It would not take me very long at all to take my things up to the Hall and then return here. You must be shaken up after you spill back there. Are you hurt in any way?'

'No Miss, really I am fine. I have a few scratches and a bruise or two but I'll be right as rain in no time. Now you go on and I'll see you shortly. Thank you again for all your help. Once I get to the Hall I will make sure that someone comes and sorts things out here proper.'

He escorted her over to her car and opened the door.

'That's very kind Bailey but as you can see this car is made for me to drive in the United States and the steering wheel is on the other side.'

'Oh yes, how silly of me, I can see that now.' Bailey closed the door again and darted around to the other side of the car and opened the door once again.

Mary-Belle Devine brushed passed him as she sat sideways in the smartly upholstered cream leather seats with red piping and then moved her shapely legs into the footwell. She rearranged her dress so that the folds sat neatly. Bailey closed the door but had a look of concern on his face.

'PC Bailey what seems to be troubling you?'

'Well Miss it's just that having the steering wheel on this side of the car must make driving in the United States very difficult. Oh well. Thank you one more time, I'm sure I will see you later once I have got a few things sorted out.'

Mary-Belle thought about informing the Policeman that Americans drove on the other side of the road but decided it was maybe just as easy to leave it. She pressed the button on the dashboard and the powerful engine fired into life. With a little effort she selected first gear and with a wave she drove off up the road in the direction of the Hall.

Bailey watched her drive away, her long hair blowing in the wind behind her. It really was a very beautiful car he thought to himself. It suited the driver perfectly....

He got his bags back together and continued his way along the road. Mary-Belle had been quite correct. The Gatehouse appeared in less than five hundred yards on the left. He remembered what Johnson had told him at the station and he passed by the gatehouse and then he entered the Motely Hall estate through the stone archway. There were large wrought iron gates here which had been opened supposedly by the gatehouse keeper to welcome in the members of the safari party. He took the right hand fork in the drive as suggested and made his way to what appeared to be the kitchens and outhouses at the rear. On his way along the side of the house, he spotted Mary-Belle's sports car parked near the stone steps which led up to the front door. There were a number of people standing around near the entrance and they were being welcomed by a rather tall thin man who Bailey assumed from the fact that he was dressed in a butler's uniform, was probably the butler.

The front door and the throng of people were lost as Bailey turned the corner and followed a low wall built of a dark brown stone in direct contrast to the attractive yellow stone of the main house. He arrived at a small iron gate. He manoeuvred the sack truck through the gate into a cobbled yard. The cobbles made any further progress with the faulty wheel impossible. Bailey stood the truck up, unfastened the leather straps and removed his bags. He continued on and up a short set of stone steps in front of him with an iron handrail to the left hand side that led to what he assumed was going to be the back door. He could hear the noises coming from the open windows. There was a wonderful smell pervading the early evening air that told him this must be the kitchen and that all manner of good things were being prepared inside for this evening's dinner. He knocked loudly on the rear door so that he might be heard above the general noise.

The door was flung open by a red faced, stout woman of perhaps forty years of age. She wore a dark blue dress with white sleeves and a large (mostly white) apron. On her head she wore a blue and white gingham cap with frills on the edges all the way around. At first she looked startled but then on seeing that the Policeman had bags with him she relaxed a little.

'Hello Madam, my name is Bailey. PC Bailey. The PC stands for Police Constable it's not my initials I would like..' but before he could say any more the lady turned and yelled over her shoulder at the top of her voice. 'Mr Crawford, I think there is someone here to see you.'

She turned her attention back to Bailey 'It is Mr Crawford that you'll be wanting sir. He is in charge you see.'

'Oh I'm sorry. Looking at you I thought that you were the cook?'

'Oh sir you are correct that I am the cook but in this house the person in charge of the kitchen is the Chef and that's who Mr Crawford is.'

She turned again and bellowed 'Mr Crawford if you have a moment, there is someone here of importance to see you!'

'I am sure you understand Constable, there is a lot to do in a kitchen when there are so many guests. Mr Crawford is very busy. You sound just my late husband with that broad Devonian accent. I haven't heard it spoken in a good long time. It brings back happy memories to me. What part are you from, I'm thinking you're from the moor?'

Bailey looked shocked for a moment. It had never occurred to him that he had much of an accent at all, so to hear that this woman thought he spoke with a broad one was quite a revelation to him. He wondered why no one back home had ever mentioned it to him. It was something he made a mental note to ask the desk sergeant about it when he returned home tomorrow.

'No madam, I'm not a moors man at all. I was born and bred in the city of Exeter. I travelled up from there this morning'

Just then, a large man dressed all in white with a large toque hat and a neckerchief appeared behind the woman. Bailey was exactly six-foot-tall but this man was a good three or four inches taller and at least four stone heavier.

'Ah you must be PC Bailey. I have been expecting you. I thought you would have been here earlier or was there a problem on the trains? That service is getting worse and worse.'

'No I caught the twelve minutes past four train from Exeter all right and the train arrived in perfect time at Midloxton Halt. However, while I was making my way here from the station, I had a small accident when I was almost run down by a runaway horse and cart. If I hadn't moved as fast as I did, I think I may have come off far worse. As it happens I have just a few cuts and bruises. Oh and that reminds me. I was able with some very kind assistance from a Miss Mary-Belle Devine who is a guest here this evening, to put the cart and the horse in a field less than half a mile down the road. Would you have someone who could go down and return them to their rightful owner?'

'Oh dear I am very sorry to hear that. I can't understand how such a thing could have happened. The men were working in the fields over the way earlier today but I can't think it was theirs because they always leave someone to look after the cart. Anyway I'll get James the stable lad to go down and sort things out, don't you worry. Now then I am Crawford the Chef here at Motley Hall. I am pleased to make your acquaintance. Well come in and don't stand on ceremony at the kitchen door any longer.'

Crawford stood back for a moment and noticed the twigs and brambles and the patch of yellow on the leg of Bailey's uniform.

'I think we better have a look at that uniform as well. We can't have you meeting her Ladyship looking like that, you would never hear the end of it, believe you me! Here give me those.'

The Chef lurched forward and took up Bailey's cases from the step and in a single motion turned and led the way through the kitchens. Motley Hall was a significant mansion house and as such the kitchen and associated rooms including the bakery and the butchery were substantial. Bailey's eyes darted around the room trying to take in the activity that was taking place. There were people everywhere stirring and chopping and peering into pans of every size and description. He kept one eye on his guide who for all his bulk seemed to dance through his team of workers as if he had second sight, gliding past precariously balanced trays of sizzling meats and then sliding past a young man stirring a liquid that bubbled slowly as his spoon made slow circles in the pot. Bailey was less deft and he collided with at least two workers on his way through.

'My apologies – pardon!'

The workers said nothing but if looks could kill Bailey knew what the outcome would have been as they steadied their precious loads from ending up on the floor or tipping over the person next to them.

Eventually they arrived at a small room off of the main kitchen. Crawford opened the door and stood to the side gesturing Bailey to go in. He did so and the big man swept in behind him and closed the door. The hubbub from the kitchen instantly reduced to a background rumble and Bailey suddenly realised just how noisy all that activity really was.

'Please take a seat there constable' Crawford indicated to a wooden chair on the far side of the room.'

Bailey sat and removed his helmet placing it on the desk in front of him. The room was quite small but had a high ceiling complete with a lantern light arrangement which made the room very light and airy in direct contrast to the hot and steamy environment which existed just outside of the door. As with the main kitchen, the walls were mainly white glazed bricks which ran floor to ceiling with a single band of dark green running around at chest height. The bricks gleamed as if someone spent a good deal of time polishing them. The room was very clean.

In direct contrast to this high level of cleanliness was the paper. There were pieces of paper everywhere, pinned in small bunches and hanging on a series of hooks that were fixed in the wall above the desk, there were piles of larger papers in three ordered sections on the desk itself and there was yet more paper on the chair that stood in front of the desk. Crawford put down the suitcase in the corner behind the door next to the hat stand and placed the smaller bag on the top. He moved to the chair and collected the paperwork up in two massive hands and deposited it with surprising dexterity to make a fourth pile in the last clear space in the middle of the desk.

'Now then constable, you must be thirsty after travelling up and then after all that has happened to you. Would you like something to drink?'

'Tea would be very nice'

'Then tea it shall be and I will have the same.' He opened the door and disappeared out of sight around the corner. In just a few moments he returned and closing the door behind him he once again created the sanctuary from the kitchen.

'I am surprised to see that you walked at all Constable, I heard that they would be sending a car for you. And then to add insult to injury, to have a horse and cart nearly run you down is bad luck. I wonder what caused it to spook like that?'

'Well Mr Crawford, as I mentioned earlier, I was helped out of my predicament by Miss Devine who fortunately was passing by in her motor car and saw the cart and then saw me in the bushes where I had landed. She turned out to be something of a horse expert, she has a number of them of her own, twenty-five I think she said, in any case she examined the horse and found that it had been shot or something in its back leg and she thinks that is what had caused the problem.'

'Shot! You mean with a gun?'

'Oh no, I should have been more clear! The horse had a small piece of metal like a dart or something stuck in its skin.'

'I see, well I would like to have a look at that myself. You see before I became a Chef I qualified as a Vet and I spent a lot of time with racehorses so I know a thing or two about how they tick.'

'Amazing. I didn't realise they did tick. Anyway so what made you give it up and become a Chef?'

Crawford looked puzzled but continued 'It was the corruption and the cruelty I couldn't take to be honest with you constable. My concern was always for the animals but often the owners and the trainers had very different agendas to me and the welfare of the horses was a long way down on theirs. I couldn't take it any more so I got out of it. I had always liked cooking and I found that I had a bit of a flair for it. I needed a job once I left the racing stable and so I signed up for three years in the army catering corps and that's where I met up with Lord Algernon Finsbury-Middlechurch who owns this place. He was a Captain and was very impressed with the food that I served up in the Officers Mess and when my time was up he offered me a job to come and work for him here as Chef at Motley-Hall and I have been here ever since.'

There was a knock at the door and a young kitchen maid brought in the tea on a tray. Bailey was delighted to see that this was tea for the workers not the upper classes. It was in big white mugs and there were two thick slices of fruit cake on some side plates and what appeared to be homemade biscuits as well.

'I didn't think you would mind a mug constable. There really isn't ever enough in those fancy little bone china cups. Help yourself to the cake and the biscuits. Rose, the woman who you met at the back door, makes the best cakes for miles around. I am rather too partial to Rose's cakes and so you would be doing me a great service if you polish them off yourself.' Crawford theatrically stuck out his stomach and patted it with his huge hands.

Bailey didn't need asking a second time and taking the top side plate he nimbly slid the largest slice of cake onto a lower plate and then helped himself to a couple of the biscuits as well. He added one spoonful of sugar and took a sip and then added two more to the tea, stirring it with a tiny silver spoon that was only just long enough to reach the bottom of the mug and settled back in his chair to sample the culinary skills of Rose the cook. He was not disappointed.

'What I wanted to ask you constable'

'Please call me John.'

'Thank you, please call me Charles. What I wanted to ask you, John, was why they have asked you to come in to look after this group. Is there anything that I need to know that I don't know? If you know what I mean?'

Bailey was lost for a minute but then rallied. 'I am here because the local Police have an important skittles match this evening. It is the Southwest finals so they are all involved in one way or another. I understand they take their skittles very seriously around here.'

'Yes they do but I am still slightly puzzled why a Policeman is needed at all. I mean are you expecting trouble of some kind?'

'Not as far as I know. It's just the skittles oh and the fact that Lady Agatha has received a few death threats...'

'What! From who? Or should I say whom?

'Ah well that's the thing. The letters weren't signed which is a real blow because if they had been that would really have helped. They all said the same thing though.'

'And what was that?'

'Um, Dear Lady Agatha, I'm going to kill you. Something like that, it's definitely a death threat.'

'Yes, yes I can see that. Oh dear well perhaps you had better waste no more time around here. Let's get you around to the front of the house and I will introduce to Burrows the Butler, come on! Oh and don't worry about your things. I will have them sent up to your room. You are staying on the first floor with the rest of the guests. I believe you are in 'Christie'.'

Bailey looked puzzled.

'That's the name of the room.'

With that Crawford was out of his seat and opening the office door. He took another route out of the kitchen and led Bailey through a scullery and then up a short flight of steps and a corridor and back to the kitchen door where he had first met Rose the cook. Crawford opened the door and continued down the steps outside into the yard and retraced the route Bailey had previously made. As they approached the corner of the house he stopped and waited for Bailey to catch up.

'Right then, I will go no further. You just walk straight up the front steps and Burrows will be there at the top.' Just then the tall figure of the Butler reappeared at the entrance door as he slowly moved back into his position on the porch to await more guests. A small party of people could be seen making their way up the driveway in the distance.

'Ah there he is, off you go constable. It has been a pleasure to meet you and I hope everything goes well for you and the guests this evening.' He extended his hand and it was then that Bailey realised he was still holding a sizable slice of cake in his hand. He looked down and then at Crawford trying to decide what to do next. He thought about giving it back but this cake was too good to give away and so he put the whole thing in his mouth, brushed his hands together and nodded at Crawford as he shook his hand.

Crawford watched as Bailey walked away and cursed as he realised he had forgotten to sort out his uniform. Oh well, too late now he thought to himself as he walked back to the organised chaos of his domain.

Bailey made it to the bottom of the main steps, his jaws working faster than his legs so that by the time he arrived at the top he was able to announce his name to Burrows. The butler really was an odd looking man. He had an inordinately long nose which was completely smooth as if there was only just enough skin to stretch over it. His overall complexion was pale and yet the very end of his nose was almost pale blue. It reminded Bailey of a picture he had seen of a mountain top and the slight dew drop that hung from the underside of the very end confirmed to

Bailey that this extremity must be cold even on a day as warm as this. His grey watery eyes were rimmed in red and they appeared to move independently of each other. Yet for all his slow, rehearsed movements he appeared to notice everything that was going on around him. He took in the dishevelled appearance of the policeman and gave an almost imperceptible sniff, the dewdrop temporarily disappeared.

'Ah yes, Police Constable Bailey. We have been expecting you. As you can see there are a number of guests imminently arriving behind you? I will need to deal with them. Perhaps you would be good enough as to make your own way into the hall and wait for me to introduce you?

Bailey nodded and walked into the hallway. Lady Agatha was the person he had been instructed to report to. He wondered what she was going to be like. Crawford had made out she was a bit of an Ogre.

He didn't have to wait long to find out.

Chapter Two

'We need an edge. Our forces are far superior to those of our enemies, however, it will become increasingly evident to them that our weakness will be in our supply lines and nowhere will we be more exposed than in the desert. It is imperative that we are in receipt of the aerial photographs of that air base which our contact in England must by now have in their possession. They will give us information of just what their capability really is and what they can send against us and in turn we will prepare for them and that will be our edge. It is our highest priority to obtain this information and believe me when I say that everyone involved in this mission is under the direct gaze of the Fuhrer himself.

This can be a very advantageous position to be in for those who succeed, but I am sure that I do not have to say that for those who fail, the consequences would be serious, very serious indeed. In short, I must have those photographs and I must have them quickly!'

General Greunig could hear his own voice rising but fought his emotions and remained calm, he knew that this tell-tale in his voice had already been picked up and processed by the person sitting so quietly facing him across his desk.

Greunig reflected how had this all come to pass? He had served his country well and as a young captain at twenty-five years old, had commanded his own unit in nineteen eighteen. After the War, he had remained in the military and his loyalty and past record had been recognised when he was promoted to the rank of General in the Fuhrer's administration.

This was not what Greunig had wanted. At forty-four years old he was truly ready for retirement but the manner in which he had been offered not only the rank but also the position as, Head of Public Works Projects, as part of the Fuhrer's four-year plan to create self-sufficiency in the Fatherland by nineteen forty, was non-negotiable. Now two years into the project, Greunig had met with much success and his improvements in the autobahn network across the country were well advanced. But he knew this plan for self-sufficiency was not just about providing employment to the workers. It was an irrefutable fact that unemployment had fallen; by the end of last year only 1 million Germans were without employment, where there had been six million in nineteen thirty-two. But there was another purpose, a sinister purpose; war!

He had wanted to turn down this position but he knew that he could not refuse. He was loyal to his country, yes, but the direction of travel which he found himself caught up in was not what he wanted to be part of. But he had to take care of his family first and foremost and to say that he didn't want this position would be seen as nothing short of desertion and an inevitable firing squad for him and possibly his loved ones as well. He pondered once more why he had been sought out for this job when there were plenty of other officers who were young rising stars, keen and loyal to the ideas of the Third Reich and all it stood for under its fanatical leader. Some of them already suspected that he did not share their faith in the Fuhrer. He suspected for the hundredth time that they were waiting for him to make a mistake and then seize their opportunity to have him removed once and for all.

And now here he was, discussing this mission with this silent, shadowy figure who he knew was analysing his every move, every aspect of his body language and his behaviour. He had to show strength, for his family he had to remain convincing. This individual was to him a very dangerous person indeed. They were a seasoned agent with many successful missions to their credit. He knew they had already killed dozens of people in cold blood, that was a given in the line of work that they were in. They survived on their instincts and their intuition. It is what gave them their edge. But more than that, this individual was a direct conduit to some of the most senior members of this administration.

Greunig was determined that this briefing would go well and he hated himself for allowing the tension to show in his voice. He wanted this agent to fear him, to carry out his instructions to the letter so that his family would survive the events that were looming larger every day with an alarming sense of inevitability.

The soft voice interrupted his thoughts.

'Forgive me Herr General, but I thought you said we already have an agent in the field with the very highest recommendations as to their credentials. Surely they should be more than able to complete this mission successfully?'

Greunig remained motionless. The sleight in that softly spoken voice had been almost imperceptible but he knew what they were saying. It was Greunig who had personally endorsed the original agent but something had gone wrong and now he found himself having to recover the situation before things got out of hand, before all hell broke loose for him. His hands curled tightly over the ends of his chair causing his fists to turn white as he channelled his frustration.

'Let us say that we are disappointed with how things have developed in the field. We expected this assignment to have been brought to a successful conclusion much earlier. You and I both know that this particular agent should have been able to obtain these photographs without any trouble at all or as the Americans would say, it should have been a walk in the park'.

'I wouldn't know about that Herr General. I do not trouble myself with trivial sayings. I understand that others were considered but that you made the final choice yourself. Is that not the case?'

Greunig chose to ignore both the put down and the question and continued.

'However, it appears that they have either developed their own agenda since they have become involved in the mission or perhaps they were always following another one. This may have been entirely of their own making or it is possible that they are working under the instruction of a party or parties that we have yet to discover. But believe me when I tell you that discover the truth we will. In any case it means that we find ourselves exposed to the very real and unwelcome risk that, should we allow the photographs to remain in the hands of this agent, they may well offer them to the highest bidder.'

There was a visible shudder from the General as he imagined in his mind's eye what the repercussions for him would be if this came to pass.

'We have already identified that the best opportunity for you to intercept the agent and obtain the photographs will be during a forthcoming social occasion which is being called 'the Last Night in England Party'. This is to be held at a manor house in the English countryside. It is a party for a group of individuals planning to embark on an expedition to Africa leaving the house on the morning of the twenty sixth and then boarding the SS Gloriana at Dover later that evening, ready to sail on the morning tide of the twenty seventh.

You are instructed to infiltrate this party and to secure the photographs.'

The General paused for a moment and retrieved a pale blue envelope for the top right hand drawer of his desk and passed it across the dark green leather top. The Eagle of the Third Reich was clearly visible in the centre.

'Here are your detailed instructions and the coded phrase that you will need to use to identify the contact. I am giving you this information because we must hope that there is still a chance that you will reach that contact ahead of the other agent. If you do, then make the transaction and withdraw from the party without the need to attract any more attention than is absolutely necessary.

However, if as we suspect, either the exchange has already taken place or you are discovered by the other agent, you know what to do.'

The envelope was picked up and placed unopened in a small leather carry case.

Greunig smiled then and visibly relaxed a little.

'You are our hope. For the record, you were always my first choice for this mission whatever you may think or have heard from others.' He lied hoping that his voice did not betray him this time.

I listened to a friend of mine who has had a long association with this agent. It was on their recommendation that I made my decision. It is a weakness I will not allow to cloud my judgement again. I now find not only that I must send you in to the field to clear things up but I must make further investigations with this friend to see if they had any involvement with the situation that has developed. I hope for their sake and for the Fatherland, that this turns out not to be the case.

Their strategic knowledge and understanding of fighting in a desert theatre will be invaluable in the times to come.

I have spoken to him and he assures me that he is as disappointed as I am that things have gone sour. I never judge a book by the cover or even by reading the first few chapters. Books have a way of hiding the truth until they reveal their true colours much later on. I will therefore reserve judgement on my opinion of what has happened here until I know the whole story.'

With that, Greunig rose from behind the table and brought the meeting to an end with a salute.

'Heil Hitler!'

The General's salute was acknowledged but not returned. The agent simply gathered their coat from the back of the chair and walked noiselessly across the thickly carpeted room to the door, opened it and was gone with just the slightest click of the latch closing behind them.

Greunig sat for a moment looking towards the door reflecting on the meeting that had just taken place and hoping against hope that this person really had the capability to retrieve the situation. He turned to the drinks cabinet to the left of the window that ran full height in this grand office of his. He liked this room and enjoyed the view over the park that the window afforded him. He poured himself a very generous scotch and then stood looking out on the scene before him. People were walking along in the early afternoon sunshine. Even though the weather was still very warm Greunig felt ice cold, mainly because he was bathed in sweat from the meeting he had just concluded. The people in the park looked normal, they went about their business completely unaware of the spectre that he could see growing above this land. He pondered for a few moments more and then decided that he needed to have an exit strategy if things went badly. His neck was on the line at the very highest level.

He needed another drink and then he needed to make some calls to make sure that if things looked bad he could disappear at a moment's notice and take his family with him. He removed the crystal stopper from the decanter and poured the liquid into his glass, he could see his own hand shaking as he poured it and decided to make this a very large one.

Chapter Three

Lady Agatha Plantagenet looked at the individuals who formed the members of the next and possibly final Safari Party and sighed to herself.

She had hoped that her usual advertisement in 'The Times' newspaper would have attracted a larger number of people in general and that hopefully within that group of respondents would have been more, who were, well how can one put this? 'Interested' in actually taking part in a Safari. Looking at her assembled group it was clear that the adventurer types were either off on other expeditions already or were perhaps just busy doing something else.

There was a strong feeling that war was just around the corner and the type of people that Agatha would have liked to have on this trip would be sought after by either side so perhaps that explained the dearth of quality adventurers as they were probably busy aligning themselves for whatever comes next. What she had been left with were, at best, keen, at worst very likely useless.

On the positive side, her nephew Monty was joining the party. Oh how she loved him and how much he reminded her of her dearly departed husband Arthur who had been such a fearless explorer across the 'dark continent' back in the day. Monty was a Major in the Hussars and a crackshot with a rifle, which she thought ought to be useful if things didn't go quite to plan. The other males making up the main party consisted of Crispin Moorcock the son of a very wealthy merchant banker who Agatha had made a mental note that he had not actually paid for his passage yet. Typical of wealthy people, she thought to herself, leaving it all to the very last moment before parting with a single penny. He didn't look like he had any idea of what was in store for him over the next few weeks and from what she had been able to gather, it was clear that the only reason he was on this trip at all was because he had got an innocent maid in the family way and his father had sent him off while he cleared up the mess left at home. Agatha was aware that there would be a good deal of exploring that would be required this time and that would mean some physical digging. Obviously she wasn't going to be able to do this manual work herself and she sorely doubted whether this Moorcock chap had ever done anything physical in his life apart from the one success with the maid.

There was also Titus of course. He was a very willing participant in the digs but he lacked any real physical strength. He was a rather small man with poor eyesight which was accentuated by his very think rimmed glasses which made his eyes appear huge. He also suffered from some sort of skin complaint which meant that he had to remain covered up from head to toe protected from the sun otherwise he suffered terribly from heat stroke and sun burn. He was however very good at organising the locals and making sure that Agatha was able to sit in the shade while overseeing the works.

The remaining members were female, one American millionairess and a writer who had already stated that the only reason she was here was for research on a book rather than the quest for treasure so it didn't bode well that either of them were likely to want to roll up their sleeves.

There were also a number of other guests attending this evening's party made up of well-wishers, a few sponsors who one must invite even though it is their money that you want not their company and a number of people who would be dropped off along the way on their own travels but who chose to travel with Agatha's group for safety in numbers and the favourable passage rates that Agatha had wrung out of the shipping line. Agatha of course added a modest percentage to their travel fees purely to cover administrative costs.

Agatha sighed again that at the very moment when she could have done with an army of workers she had been deserted. This trip was so very important because with all that was happening in Europe and the very real prospect of another war looming, it was very unlikely she would be able to make this trip again anytime soon, if indeed ever again, depending on the outcome of the hostilities. She needed to bring back a decent haul of Egyptian antiquities otherwise life in her old age was not going to be anywhere near as comfortable as she was hoping. She had a number of buyers, mainly Americans, lined up who were very keen to part with their cash for anything with provenance from Egypt. Agatha had established herself as the leading authority on all things Egyptian and so anything that she offered for sale was quickly snapped up without too many difficult questions being asked.

Agatha was more than aware that the Egyptian authorities were becoming inquisitive about the fact that they had given her a free rein on excavations in and around the tombs on the basis that she had agreed to return anything she found of significance to them. However the amount of treasure that they had received seemed to be at odds to the amount of feverish work that went on during these digs. The Government had decided to try and find out what was going on themselves and had sent in spies to mix with the locals. During a number of 'conversations' with the workers recruited by Agatha, or to be perfectly accurate more often by

Titus on her behalf, they had been very clear with their information, or might we more correctly say confessions, that certain pieces had been discovered and yet these never appeared on any inventory.

The Inspector of archaeological excavations Mustafa Faziel had received a memo from the Minister of the Interior instructing him, in very clear terms, that he really should pay more visits and more attention to the workings during the forthcoming dig and that perhaps he ought to stay around for a few days instead of retiring for a very lavish luncheon provided by Lady Agatha on the very first afternoon and then returning to his office for the duration thereafter.

In short, Agatha knew that time was running out.

*

Motley Hall, she reflected, had been a good choice, the venue was very well appointed and what is more, as the place was owned by her distant cousin Lord Algernon Finsbury-Middlechurch, it had cost her nothing at all to use it. Oh she knew that when Algy had said 'why not pop down and visit me and we can talk about these expeditions that you go on?' She knew that he hadn't really offered his house for the 'Last Night In England Party' but sometimes you had to seize on an opportunity when it was offered no matter how vague or innocent that offer might have been, carpe diem and all that!

'Well you know Algy this really is very, very good of you to offer Motley Hall like this, overly generous really but how could I refuse? Oh no, there is no point in saying it is nothing because it is, it really is. I will make sure that all of the family know just how good you have been about all of this. I think that is the least I can do because you know, and I don't like to gossip, there are some members of the family that have always seen you as a bit of a fool. No perhaps fool is not the word but a bit of a soft touch, yes perhaps that is a better phrase altogether but I can tell you that I shall be putting them right on that point. In simple terms dear boy, you are nothing short of a knight in shining armour because when you discovered that your favourite Aunty Agatha was without anywhere to hold her famous 'last night' party and more importantly that your favourite Aunty Agatha had no money whatsoever to pay for said party. It was you who stepped to the fore and offered this marvellous home of yours, Motley Hall.'

Agatha smiled inwardly. She could see the utter bewilderment on her poor cousin's face as he tried to stutter his way through a protest. But the poor man had been outgunned and outmanoeuvred by a master. Not only was he stuck with having his Aunt, and he was sure that during his childhood he had only ever seen her once and couldn't quite understand how she had become his 'favourite'. But worse still he found himself packed off to his London home in Belgravia for the weekend leaving Agatha with complete control of the house and a number of his household staff already considering alternative employment.

The guests had had a chance to settle into their rooms and were now assembling in the Great Hall sipping their pre-dinner drinks. Agatha decided it was time she should welcome everyone. At the end of the Great Hall, the room Burrows the butler had informed her was most commonly used for large dining events here at Motley Hall, was a double staircase that met with a landing with the main entrance leading off from there. The landing held a commanding position over the room and it was from here that Agatha decided she would rally her troops, such as they were.

As she walked up the short flight to the landing she was interrupted by Titus calling to her in a loud whisper 'Um Agatha, I assume you are about to welcome everyone so you might want my latest information on our travel arrangements for the morning.'

Agatha halted her progress on the stairs and turned to address her assistant 'Ah yes Titus that would be most useful, we have already had more than one false start concerning in which port we might find our ship so it will be good to at least get the start right!'

Agatha continued to the landing well aware that Titus would hurry along to join her and she wasn't disappointed on this occasion as she heard him begin his ascent behind her. 'Well Agatha, it would appear that actually neither of us is correct. As you know I had gathered from the information I was given that we would join the ship at Southampton while your information seemed to suggest that we would make our way from Dover. In fact, from the latest conversation that I have just had with the shipping company it now looks as if Portsmouth is where we will be embarking.'

'Portsmouth, are you quite sure Titus?'

'Indeed I am Lady Agatha. I have just got off the telephone from talking to the booking office for the East India Company and they are adamant that this is the case. They apologise for any inconvenience that this might have caused and they assure me that they sent a telegram to our London residence yesterday unaware that we had already left on our journey here to Motley Hall.'

'Well then Titus, this is very opportune that we have this information to hand. I am indeed about to address our guests as is customary at the beginning of our little parties. I think it is important that I set out in as much detail as one can without wanting to scare people off before they have even left these shores, what they might expect over the forthcoming weeks. You know Portsmouth always holds such fond memories for me. I have spent many an evening with the boys on the waterfront.'

Agatha drifted off for as moment with a wistful look on her face clearly enjoying her happy memories of days long gone by before she returned to the task at hand.

'Very well Titus we will go with your latest news and hope that the dear man at the East India booking office does indeed have his facts correct.'

Chapter Four

'To be honest with you Moorcock, my aunt, Lady Agatha Plantagenet has never really had very much time for any her relatives. In fact, after the passing of her husband, my uncle Arthur, the only one of them that she even vaguely likes, appears to be me. My name is Montague but she has always insisted on calling me Monty. You asked me what I do. Well old boy, if you haven't already guessed from the uniform, I am an officer in the Hussars.

In fact, our family has a deep rooted military history, you can look back over the extensive Fortescue-Smythe family tree and you would find at least one relative that was in the armed forces for the last two hundred years. It's in our blood. My childhood up until the age of eleven was spent in Delhi where my father was a Colonel in the Indian Army and was based at The Army in India Headquarters (A.H.Q. India). Later on father accepted the posting of Temporary Brigadier which also had the dual responsibility of General Officer Commanding British Troops in the Sudan based in Khartoum. This was a significant promotion as the position commanded one Colonel and fourteen other officers to assist him.

I thoroughly enjoyed living in Khartoum for almost ten years but the Officer Training School at Sandhurst finally beckoned as I knew it would when I reached the age of twenty-one. Two years later I passed out of Sandhurst with the highest marks of my year including being undefeated as marksman during my time there.

I then had a real purple patch and rose through the ranks at a fairly rapid pace. I was twice decorated for bravery shown in the heat of battle in the Great War. To be honest I don't remember being particularly brave. It was just something that one had to get on with at the time. However, some bright spark seemed to have jotted down my exploits and reported them and the next thing I know the top brass had me up on parade and I got a bally medal don't you know. Anyway I am now on the brink of probably my final posting to India and have decided to travel over to Africa with Aunty on this expedition before joining my new battalion in Delhi.

You know if you listen to Aunt Agatha, she will tell you that I am the spitting image of her husband Arthur, as a young man, and that is probably the main reason why she likes me. I assume that I remind her of the love of her life.

For my part I have had a very fortunate upbringing and being a decorated soldier in a bright red uniform does wonders with the ladies.

But in answer to the second part of your question, no Moorcock old man, I am not along on this safari in any sort of security or indeed military capacity at all. Of course, I will be bringing my rifle and sidearm but that is because there is always a possibility that I might get a chance to take a pot-shot at something. Naturally if there is any trouble then I will be able to defend myself and the rest of the party but I am sure there won't be any need. I would look a lot nearer than Africa if its trouble that's your worry.'

'Yes, I see what you are saying; the unrest in Europe is certainly most concerning. My father has made it clear to me that war will make some people very rich and bankers such as my father are clever men who are well placed. All the same I think it is comforting to know that I will not be the only person on this trip who can shoot straight should the need arise'

'You Moorcock? I had no idea; well yes I would certainly be able to shoot straight. Now why don't I freshen up that gin and tonic before dinner for you and then you can tell me all about your sharpshooter adventures. I have to say old man you don't look the type, no offence of course.' Monty picked up Crispin Moorcock's glass and moved away towards the bar. On his way he moved right into the path of Edith Marrowbone.

'Ah Miss Marrowbone, delighted to bump into you, so to speak. I haven't had much chance to talk to you yet but I have always been very interested in the idea of writing something and so you interest me very much.'

Edith could see that this man was clearly making what in her opinion was a very lame attempt at a pass. She was still new to the idea that men found her attractive. She had often felt in her formative years that she was going to be overlooked, an old maid left on the shelf. But she had changed, she knew she had and this was just another reminder of that fact. She had always had a good figure but she had made little attempt to show it off, choosing to concentrate on her writing more than anything else. Even now she wore her hair in a tight plait on the top of her head. But with her new found wealth she had taken a look around and noted what other women wore and had simply copied them. It had been a very successful transformation and she had received more than her fair share of compliments from both sexes.

Tonight she had chosen a formal black dress, quite understated really with a large peacock brooch pinned below her left shoulder which caught the light beautifully. It wasn't particularly expensive and contained mainly small garnets rather than diamonds but it had been given to her by someone who meant a great deal to her and so she liked to wear it near to her heart. Had this been a ball or some charity dinner event, both of which she seemed of late to be invited to with alarming regularity, she would have probably ignored him completely. But the night was young and she knew that she was going to be in the close company of this man for the next few weeks so why start off on the wrong foot?

'Well that's lovely to hear Major and call me Edith please. I would be delighted to talk to you, at some length, about my writing and perhaps you could regale me about your travels around the world and your brave deeds. I did a little reading about my fellow travelling partners who are coming on this trip and I was interested to read that you have been decorated on two occasions for bravery.'

The Major lifted his shoulders in a gesture of dismissal but she continued before he could speak.

'Now I know that you are going to say that it was nothing but we both know that it is in the nature of the true hero to dismiss the act of bravery as if it were all in a day's work and that anyone else would have done the same thing given the same set of circumstances, am I correct?'

'You are very perceptive Edith; that was more or less exactly what I was going to say. Look I am going to spruce up this G&T for Moorcock. I was going to hear about his acts of bravery but to be honest when I mentioned that I would like to hear all about them, he had a look on his face that told me his stories were likely to be just that, stories. And anyway I would very much like to continue this conversation with you. So if you will just excuse me for a moment'.

Edith was about to tell him to hurry back when she noticed the figure of Lady Agatha entering the room through the large doors that opened into the West corridor. She took one more glance in the direction of Monty and then decided to mingle with some other guests who were nearby.

On returning with the drinks, the Major was disappointed to see that Edith had disappeared however his spirits were soon lifted as he looked over in the direction of Moorcock to see that he was talking to Mary-Belle Devine a dear friend of Monty's for over four years, having first met up at a polo match in Windsor when she was accompanied by her husband Dwight Devine. He had subsequently met Mary-Belle alone on a number of occasions and it would be safe to say they now had a 'special' relationship. Mary-Belle caught his eye and she smiled one of those smiles that really lit up her face. She quickly made her excuses and left Moorcock's company. She walked slowly and deliberately towards Monty trying to fix his gaze, almost daring him to look anywhere but directly at her. But Monty was a confident man and he enjoyed watching her body as she made her way across the space in between them like a big cat stalking its prey. He liked her a lot, he had done so from the moment he had first seen her. She had that effect on most men and he knew that she was more than aware of that fact.

As he looked past her he could see Moorcock taking a good look as Mary-Belle walked away from him, Monty couldn't resist the opportunity to raise his hand and fake a shot at Crispin with his make believe cowboy gun hand. He blew the smoke away from the end of the pretend barrel and re-holstered his gun just like the sheriff always did after shooting the gunslinger. He grinned at the expression of panic on the face of Crispin. He knew he would have to speak to this banker's son again, somewhere quiet away from all of these people. But before he could think any more about that important meeting, his thoughts were pleasantly interrupted by the arrival of Mary-Belle Devine.

'I didn't see you come in Monty, I was beginning to believe that you were going to let me down'.

'Have I ever let you down dear lady since our first meeting?'

'On the contrary, you have always been very attentive. But I know that you have things to do. To most people you are a soldier but I know that is only part of your life'.

'Mary-Belle I have told you before, there are times and there are places to have these conversations and this is not one of them. There is someone here that I will need to meet privately. You may be of some assistance in making that meeting happen but I have to tell you it is not without danger.'

'Let us not forget Major, that half of the developed world believes that I killed my dear husband Dwight on our yacht for his money. If that is to be believed, then it is you that might be the one in danger don't you think?' Mary-Belle threw her head back laughing at her own joke. Her hair moved away slightly from her neck and Monty could just see for an instant the small scar where her husband's knife had nicked the skin, just an inch away from her carotid artery. The incident had happened during one of his many bouts of drunkenness which always ended in a foul argument. He had thrown the knife as a last ditch attempt to stop her leaving the house that night. It had the required effect. She remained and he, full of guilt, tended her injury. Had the cut been just an inch away the outcome of that evening would have been very different. Now Monty remembered how he had first discovered the scar and how he had kissed it on many occasions since.

'Yes perhaps it is me that is in danger though I recall that there was more than one newspaper that tied us together as we had been seen out together on two occasions in public alone and they made the suggestion that perhaps I too was somehow involved in the death of your husband. It was far-fetched even in its suggestion and I was able to quash the rumour very quickly as I was on a diplomatic mission in Sweden with the Foreign Secretary at the exact same time you were on your yacht off the Florida Coast. To read the articles, you would have thought we were Bonnie and Clyde!'

They both laughed together, perhaps with a little too much enthusiasm but no-one around them saw anything out of place.

'If you need me to help you with anything at all my lovely man you know you only have to ask. I will see you after dinner perhaps and then we have that lovely crossing on the ship to make tomorrow. I am sure there will be a number of opportunities for us to reacquaint ourselves of each other?'

'Indeed there will be but for now I must go and talk to my Aunt'

'And I must try and catch up with that vicar, I understand that he is allocating berths, I must make sure mine is a double room with a decent sized bath!'

Monty went to walk away from Mary-Belle but then caught her arm and said gently 'for the purpose of this evening I will spend the rest of the time rather drunk. Don't ask why please just accept it.'

She nodded and moved off in search of the little clergyman.

Monty turned around to confront whoever might be in earshot and with a loud voice exclaimed; 'This champagne is marvellous. I suggest we all drink as much of it as we can this evening because it is very unlikely that they are going to have anything as good as this in Africa!'

Chapter Five

Her choice to wear the full length beaded dress that accentuated all her curves and none of her edges had been a good one. As she surveyed the room it was clear to Mary-Belle Devine that, as usual, she had captured the attention of all of the men in the room and from their shocked expressions, a great many of the women as well. It was a strange phenomenon mused Mary-Belle as she stood there with her perfect pout and even more perfectly white teeth, how even though her dress was of the deepest pink, the colour that she saw reflected in most of the women faces in the room was much closer to the colour of her own eyes which were green.

Mary-Belle was pleased with her entrance and with the effect that her outrageously expensive attire had caused. Yes, this dress was a lot of money but then when you find yourself the sole beneficiary of your husband's Will which amounts to almost one hundred and eighty million US dollars, then you find that you can 'splash the cash' without too much concern...and Mary- Belle could really 'splash'.

Before her marriage to Dwight Devine, she had been used to a much more conventional lifestyle. If you could ever engage her in a conversation about her youth, you would learn from her own mouth that she was the only child of Michael and Frances Dooley who were second generation Irish immigrants who had made good through the hard work and careful planning of their own parents.

Mary-Belle's paternal Grandfather Padraic had arrived in the United States as an immigrant from a tiny area just outside of Waterford called Ballyogarty in Ireland and had scratched a living out of the Arizona dust until one day after listening to a travelling preacher and taking the words of the good Lord to his soul, Padraic had become a preacher himself and found that that he was good at it and that people listened.

In a short space of time he transformed from the stooped figure of a migrant worker to a man who stood upright and talked the word of God from the pulpit and from the stage and from every other vantage point where he could stand and be heard. The news of his success reached the Towns and then the Cities and he was brought into them to preach and with the success came the money. And Padraic Dooley knew that he must use this money from God to give his only son Michael a better start in this promised land of America and so he encouraged him first into college and then through law school to better himself.

It was while he was studying Law at Harvard that Michael had met Frances Mulligan-Mulvaney whose family has also emigrated from Ireland during 'an Gorta Mór' (The Great Famine) and had gone West seeking the land of gold only to find that the gold was hidden deep underground and everyone was trying to dig it out with little regard to life or limb. Frances's father Kevin Mulligan had been a giant of a man who knew how to manage men and he surrounded himself with a team of labourers who he hired out as workers.

When the gold ran out, he moved his men into construction and worked hard to build his business into the eighth largest construction company in the United States. He provided for his family and even though he worked long hours he would always ask Frances on a Sunday morning, as the family made ready for Church, how she was doing with her studies and to name him two things that she had learned that week. If she couldn't name two new things, then it was a very long wait for a very small Sunday lunch for her and then early to bed for a week. One of the many things she definitely learned early on was to make sure that she always had two new things for her father every week! The learning paid off and Frances got a good job, for a young woman, as a researcher at Harvard College where she met Michael, they fell in love and they married in the last days of a New England Summer in nineteen ten, but they had to wait five long years before they were blessed with their first child, a daughter, Mary in the October of nineteen fifteen. Mary received a good Catholic upbringing and was educated at the exclusive Corpus Christie College on the outskirts of Seattle where the family had moved after Michael had secured a good position as a junior partner in a law firm specialising in corporate cases. He was already showing promise. Mary completed her education in nineteen thirty-two, spending a year at a Swiss finishing school. But Mary could see that there were lots of young girls who spoke well and she knew that she needed to stand out from the crowd if she was going to get anywhere. So she changed her name to Mary-Belle in nineteen thirty-four and acquired the cutest southern drawl you ever heard and when she walked into the life of Dwight Devine the oil billionaire in the autumn of that year – he didn't stand a chance.

*

Mary-Belle looked over to the centre of the room and saw PC Bailey still covered in some of the hay and hedgerow from his earlier encounter. She smiled to herself as the poor man was clearly getting a dressing down from Lady Agatha. She decided to intervene on his behalf.

'Why hello there PC Bailey, I do hope that you are none the worse for wear after your unfortunate accident earlier?'

'Oh Miss Devine. How lovely to see you again. No I am more or less unscathed, apart from the bits that got the worst of the brambles....those bits are fairly scathed to be honest and they are really going to smart when I get some iodine on them!'

Lady Agatha, somewhat taken aback that this beautiful woman appeared to be on such good terms with a bumbling Policeman who she had thought to have just arrived, turned to face Mary-Belle.

'Ah you are clearly Miss Mary-Belle Devine. I have heard much about you my dear but I didn't know that you were an acquaintance of the local constabulary?' enquired Lady Agatha looking over her half- rimmed spectacles.

'I'm not actually that local to be honest Lady Agatha' Bailey chimed in.

'There is no need to bother with details Bailey. Miss Devine understands exactly to what I refer when I say local constabulary, so please do not interrupt.'

Bailey made to make his reply but was saved when Mary-Belle interjected, 'Oh yes it is true Lady Agatha. I had the pleasure of meeting PC Bailey earlier this afternoon. I was on my way here in my automobile when I came around a bend in the road to be confronted with the sight of a horse and cart that had clearly come to rest at the side of the road. I immediately stopped to see what had happened to the driver and it was then that I saw the unfortunate constable in the bushes'.

'Why does that not surprise me?' snorted Lady Agatha.

Mary-Belle continued 'well I helped him gain his footing again and he climbed out of the hedgerow. I then went over and inspected the horse which thankfully appeared no worse for wear for the ordeal apart from being very distressed. We looked around and decided to place the horse and cart in a nearby field and that is where we have left it. I asked PC Bailey to arrange for a member of staff to send someone down from here to return the horse and cart to its rightful owner'.

'Indeed. It would appear you are very resourceful Miss Devine, which may come in very useful on our forthcoming trip. There are often times when things cannot be done by the staff and we need everyone's efforts and ingenuity to achieve our aims'.

'And what exactly are our aims on this trip Lady Agatha? I am interested to find out. I have really only signed up out of boredom. You are probably aware that I have been fortunate to inherit a great deal of money from the untimely death of my husband which caused me a great deal of sorrow and more than my fair share of attention from the press. I saw this trip as a chance to get away from everyone who knows me for a while.'

Bailey looked into the face of Mary-Belle Devine as he had earlier in the day and he couldn't help but notice her loveliness all over again. He observed her closely for a few moments and noted that, although she talked fondly of her late husband, no tears began to well in those beautiful eyes which struck him as odd given his very recent demise.

'The discovery of treasure and its safe return to England of course. That must be our primary aim. It is our duty dear lady to ensure that we rescue it from the grasp of the Germans.' With that Lady Agatha threw Mary-Belle a look that would have withered dried flowers and moved off to find some other poor unsuspecting victims.

'So PC Bailey, we meet again. I guess that even though you had a bit of an unfortunate accident on the way here, now that you have arrived, you are really the main guy in charge of things, is that right?' Mary-Belle had moved closer to the constable and gently brushed the last remaining evidence of his earlier encounter with the local flora away.

'Ah well in a manner of speaking I am' he stammered 'Of course I am only here to carry out the function of crowd control because it was thought that, given the death threats, there might be persons yet unknown who might want to harm Lady er..' Bailey stopped in mid-sentence, he had said too much and he knew it. The problem was he found this woman very easy to talk to and his mouth had run away with itself. Mary-Belle naturally responded to this news.

'There have been death threats? I wasn't aware of anything like that. Oh my! That does put a different angle of things. I had wondered why such a small gathering in the countryside should attract the presence of a policeman. I thought for a while that it was just a quaint little thing that you all do over here for titled Lords and Ladies but then I thought maybe it wasn't just because of her title but maybe because Lady Agatha was well connected perhaps with the authorities. It seems I am wrong on both counts. I now see that the reason you are here PC Bailey is because of something far more serious going on in the background that most of the people on this trip are probably completely unaware of.'

'Oh no, Miss Devine, I shouldn't really have mentioned that at all. You are in fact correct when you say that Lady Agatha is well connected. Her very good friend is Inspector Lansdowne of Scotland Yard and that is partly the reason why a police officer has been sent along. We would always take death threats very seriously of course but given the sensitive

46

times in which we all find ourselves is the real reason why I am here. I would sooner that you don't make it general knowledge to everyone here if that is all right with you miss? I wouldn't want to alarm anyone untowardly by thinking that perhaps their life is in danger because of some madman that could be lurking in our midst.'

'Madman! Oh dear me this really sounds bad PC Bailey, then these threats have obviously been very serious indeed?'

'I am not making a very good job of explaining the situation at all. Please be assured Miss Devine that you are in no danger. The fact of the matter is that there have been a couple of letters written to Lady Agatha which caused her to contact her good friend Inspector Lansdowne who said that he would make sure that he sent someone along just to keep an eye out, nothing more than that, really nothing more at all Miss.'

'Well if you're sure PC Bailey', Mary-Belle moved close to his ear. Bailey could smell her exquisite perfume pervading his nostrils, 'then just make sure that you stay close is that all right?'

Mary-Belle collected a glass of champagne from a passing waiter and glided away. For a moment PC Bailey stood where he was and wondered exactly what had just happened. She smiled to herself; she knew the effect that she was having on him; it was the same with most men. A feeling that washed over even good family men as, for just the brief time they spent in her company, thoughts of their wives were moved to the farthest recesses of their consciousness, and dangerous, unpredictable and exciting thoughts that lay dormant in these good men, though never far from the surface all the same, came alive for a few brief moments.

She allowed herself one more moment of her thoughts to dwell on the constable. She doubted when Inspector Lansdowne had assured his dear friend Agatha that he would send a Police presence to attend her little gathering, that it would be in the form of the very sweet but totally incompetent PC Bailey.

Chapter Six

'It isn't my fault Lady Agatha! It was very clear on the documentation that I showed you last week that the ship would be leaving from Southampton. You thought on the other hand that we would be sailing from Dover and as I mentioned earlier to you I have confirmed that it is now most definitely Portsmouth'.

'There you go again Titus, getting things wrong. I don't understand how you could have made such an error. Mind you, now that the opportunity to discuss things has arisen, I need to mention that this isn't the only thing that you have made a mistake with in the last couple of months. Are you feeling quite all right?'

'Quite all right thank you Lady Agatha.'

'Yes at least the last couple of months I should say, if asked of course, I naturally wouldn't just come out with such a comment as an idle remark that one might make over dinner. Oh dear me no. It is particularly vital that the members of this party perceive us as a strong team. We can show no cracks in the organisation of the trip, we must appear meticulous, fully attentive, 'on the money' so to speak, otherwise we shall lose them before we even get to port and we shall need every last one of them to be involved when we reach the Valley of the Kings if we are to be successful in our endeavours Titus.'

'Oh yes indeed Lady Agatha, I fully understand.'

'Make no mistake; this will undoubtedly be our last trip to Egypt for the time being. In fact, depending on the outcome of Mr Hitler's efforts, it could be that this is our final trip, ever!'

'Surely you cannot think like that Lady Agatha! The Allies must prevail in the end. I agree that this could be our last venture for a while but eventually we shall win. After all God is on our side!'

'I wonder what you think the German clergy are telling their boys hmmmm?' she replied.

'Yes I have often pondered that thought myself Lady Agatha.'

'And what have you concluded Titus? I am interested to hear your solution to this conundrum.'

'My conclusion is that my German counterparts provide comfort in the same way that I do. Every man must believe that the Lord is on their side otherwise they would not have the strength to face their enemy. I believe that God is looking out for the German troops as well. It is their leader who he has turned his back on and in time the people of Germany will see this and then he will fall!'

Lady Agatha turned to look at her assistant. His face showed someone who truly believed everything they had just spoken. In fact the usually timid Titus had the look of a man with conviction, the look of a man who had just delivered this speech from his pulpit and whose congregation sat transfixed, their upturned faces as one, focussed on said pulpit as if the very vision of the fires of hell had just been delivered unto them and that all were convinced beyond any doubt that molten lava was about to erupt forth upon the sinners amongst them.

'You know Titus, there is a side to you I clearly have never really known. You look simple enough most of the time and yet you come out with a speech like that completely out of the blue.'

Lady Agatha turned and walked away leaving Titus fussing with his papers.

'I'll make the arrangements for the journey to Portsmouth straight away Lady Agatha.'

But Lady Agatha was already not listening to Titus. She was mulling over how much her assistant had changed since returning from his last trip to Casablanca. She also made a mental note to telephone her friend Inspector Lansdowne in the morning to see if there was anything further he might be able to find out about the mysterious fire at Stanton Drew Rectory where Titus had been working before he became her assistant. It was always a good thing to be prepared for any eventuality she thought.

Titus watched Lady Agatha leave through the doors at the end of the corridor. For a moment he heard the sounds of laughing and the general drone generated by chit chat mixed in with the sounds of fine glassware chiming together. The pre-dinner drinks reception was seemingly going very well. Titus was looking forward to dinner. He hoped it would be something very nice and very filling. For such a small man he had an insatiable appetite. The door closed behind her and the corridor fell quiet once more. With Lady Agatha out of sight he slumped onto a nearby stool and took a clean handkerchief from his cassock pocket and wiped the beads of sweat that he could feel had formed on the back of his neck.

That was too close for comfort he thought to himself. Agatha was starting to ask too many questions for his liking. He knew he had to focus, there was a lot riding on this and he had to make sure that he got this right. He would be contacted soon enough he thought. But what then, could he really go through with this? It had all seemed such a good idea, an easy way to get some real money behind him and then he could consider a new start. But now it was far less clear. His actions and the outcome of them would be significant either way.

Titus collected his thoughts and moved back into the dining room. He casually glanced around the room and caught the eye of Major Fortescue-Smythe who moved over to him.

'Ah Reverend Jennings, I have just spoken with my Aunt and it appears that you almost made a complete ass of yourself by sending us all to the wrong port! It won't do old chap; it won't do at all. That sort of mistake would never happen in the Army. Civilians are just so slapdash.'

'Yes indeed Major, I can see how you would think that. I think I am sitting over there on table six, have you checked the seating plan to see where you will be seated once the pre-dinner drinks have finished? Of course before I get to sit down I have a task to perform. I am saying the Grace you know.'

'Well I would rather imagine that you would do man, you are the vicar after all. Just make sure you get that right eh!?' barked the Major and heartily slapped Titus on his back nearly sending him into a waiter who was carrying a tray of crystal glasses from the kitchen. The waiter was fortunately a seasoned campaigner who recovered his composure and continued on his way though not before the people on the nearest table had taken a sharp intake of breath anticipating the worse.

Chapter Seven

'Well, you see the thing is Father thought that it would be a good idea if I went away for a bit. In the meantime, he said that he would find somewhere else for this maid thing to go. Definitely for the best, Father says so and he really knows what he is talking about. He is after all very rich.'

Crispin Moorcock was talking socially to an assembled group of people and to the untrained eye that was exactly what he was doing. But if you stopped and looked for more than a moment you would observe that what he was really doing was talking at them about himself, very intensely it has to be said, but talking at them he most definitely was. In fact, once you had made this discovery the longer you observed the more you could see that he was laying out the story of his reason for being here and that the events leading to him needing to be here were really none of his doing and most definitely not his fault. He truly believed that he was the injured party.

At five foot ten, he was above average height with a shock of blonde hair that he wore slicked down with a side parting on the left hand side. The front fringe was swept back giving him a dashing look, and from the attention that he received from his lady admirers, he thought he had got his look right. The thought had never occurred to him that it had more to do with his frightfully proper English accent and the fact that he regularly name-dropped his rich friends and the fact that his father was a millionaire banker. Most women found these attributes far more attractive than his looks and enabled them to overlook the fact that he was, at best, an immature upper class twit. As the old saying goes, 'there is no such thing as an ugly millionaire'.

The fact that some poor young woman who had taken him his breakfast tray and had woken him softly from his sleep and then, as he had found himself 'in the mood', had taken advantage of his position as the only son and heir of the wealthy banker Jacob Moorcock and reminded her of her position as a housemaid. The result was that she was now carrying his child and to Crispin, well that was really all a bit 'inconvenient'.

His father Jacob, had hurriedly arranged for his 'idiot of a son', a reference he found he sadly used more often than not to describe Crispin's behaviour these days, to join this safari trip to get him out of the way while he 'cleared up the mess' left behind.

Thankfully, for the maid, Jacob Moorcock was a man of high morals and principles and there was no question in his mind that this unfortunate girl should be turned out in disgrace. Instead, he instructed his housekeeper, a kindly woman named Mrs Holden, to arrange for the young woman to be relocated in a house that he owned by the seaside in Bexhill-on-Sea. She would move there with the credible story that she was a young woman whose dear husband had been killed in a terrible accident after they had been married for less than a year and now she was left in this condition. This would guarantee that the local community looked kindly on her and she would be welcomed in. She would also receive an allowance of five hundred pounds per year from a Trust that Jacob would set up in her name.

Crispin would know nothing of any of this of course and to be honest his father doubted if he had the mental capacity to understand why it had all been arranged in the first place. Crispin only really operated on one level and that was to socialise with people he perceived as being of an equal social standing as himself. The others, the 'working class' people, were just people who one needed to do things for you and they really had no other purpose.

He was staggeringly selfish, self-opinionated, conceited and oblivious to what really happened in the world outside of his cosseted and thoroughly spoilt existence.

Of course, to his perceived equals, he was a charming individual who could regale stories of his life, his bravery (completely false but handy when trying to impress a woman) and of course his wealth.

So now, here he was about to embark on a journey half way around the world. He had travelled before, skiing in the Alps every year since he was ten years old and lately three business trips with his father to New York. On each occasion every last detail of the trip had been taken care of for him, so it was all very annoying that this vicar chappie had turned up in front of him saying….

'I do apologise for this Mr Moorcock but there appears to be a problem with your payment for the forthcoming safari'.

'Well what exactly do you mean?' said Crispin, trying very hard not to show his annoyance as he had spotted a delightful woman coming down the staircase in a stunning pink beaded dress and he didn't want to miss the opportunity of talking to her as soon as possible.

'The problem is Mr Moorcock that we haven't received a penny and Lady Agatha is very strict on non-payers. Her motto has always been "in God we trust, everyone else pays cash up front"'.

'I see, how very quaint. Well you can't think for a moment that I am not good for the money. You do realise who my father is? He is Jacob Moorcock. He is a prominent merchant banker. His word is as good as cash itself and I am rather annoyed that we are even having this conversation, in fact my dear little man in God you may trust because he probably banks with my father!'

Titus looked at the man with an open mouth only half believing what he had just heard this young man say. He could see that Crispin Moorcock was not about to rescind it and so he changed his tack.

'Mr Moorcock I was merely pointing out that a payment has not been received as yet and I wanted to let you know because I didn't want you to be caused any embarrassment tomorrow when we join the ship'.

'Oh yes I see, well then I suppose I should be grateful to you, I will telephone my father as soon as I have an opportunity and sort it out. Now I really must catch up with that lady over there, I think she is an old friend of the family but for the life of me I can't remember her name. I don't suppose you know it do you Jennings?' Moorcock extended a finger in the direction of the vision in pink he had spotted earlier.

'That would be Miss Mary-Belle Devine Mr Moorcock'.

'Ah yes that's right Mary-Belle and Miss you said, how splendid, how perfectly splendid'. Moorcock moved off making a beeline for Miss Devine. She was already engaged in a conversation but that was of no consequence and he was soon engrossed in her every word, Titus Jennings and any problems with payments long forgotten.

'So Miss Devine tell me how you come to be joining this safari party, are you perhaps one of the sponsors?'

'Why no Mr Moorcock, I am actually one of the members of Lady Agatha's party as indeed I understand you are. We will be digging together in the Valley of the Kings, just think about that for a moment, all dusty together....'

'I say that sounds jolly exciting doesn't it? Though to be honest Miss Devine, it is still Miss isn't it?' Mary- Belle nodded. 'Splendid, I um actually didn't really intend to do much in the way of um digging as it were. I was going to take a more observational hands-off type of stance. Sort off let the staff and locals do the physical stuff so to speak um really', Moorcock saw the look of disappointment in Mary-Belle's expression and quickly interjected, 'But, but now that you come to mention it I think it would um indeed be great er sport I mean fun, yes that's it fun to actually, physically do something er physical wouldn't it?' He beamed his best smile in her direction hopeful that he hadn't blown his chances with this delightful woman before he had even had a chance to buy her some champagne which always impressed the ladies.

Mary-Belle smiled and gently touched his arm. 'Then I am looking forward to this safari more than I thought I was going to. I had really only joined because I needed to get away from all of the publicity over the death of my poor husband but enough of that, let us enjoy our drinks and then dinner I am sure that we will talk again Crispin.'

Crispin smiled as Mary-Belle ended their conversation. He watched her walk away and suddenly sensed that he the watcher was being watched. He turned his attention away from the disappearing sashaying rear view of Mary-Belle Devine and looking beyond her he found the face of Major Monty Fortescue -Smythe looking straight at him. He had already had a brief conversation with the Major earlier and had decided that he wasn't someone he wanted to spend a great deal of time with. He was all guns and bravado and the problem was Monty's bravado was probably real whereas Crispin's only really existed in his mind. He didn't want to have to get into any deep questioning over events with the Major otherwise things might start to get a little sticky. As Crispin stared across at Monty, the Major grinned and raised his arm in front of him like a pistol and pretended to shoot him. He then raised the tip of his finger and blew the imaginary smoke away just like children did when they played cowboys and Indians. Monty brought his hand back down to his side but continued to grin, though now the expression was more like a sneer. What a very strange action thought Crispin as he turned away, why on earth would the Major have done that? Crispin Moorcock thought for a moment and then lost himself in another conversation putting on the front once again, blah blah blah, but his mind continued to work in the background while his mouth continued to work on auto pilot. Had Monty discovered that he was on to him? That wasn't possible surely, he had been very careful. He would need to keep a close eye on him from now on. Nothing must go wrong, nothing at all.

Chapter Eight

'Well it would be true to say that my books have sold very well, so if that is a measure for success then I am indeed a successful writer. However, for me it is more that I am able to tell my stories, to share the passion of my writing, rather than the money'.

Edith Marrowbone replied to the question posed by the woman who was clearly after an autograph, as she stood at the entrance to Motley Hall.

The small woman in the fox fur coat looked confused. She was an autograph collector and her experiences of obtaining autographs from the great and the good had taught her that if you compliment your target and pander to their success, you were much more likely to get the desired result. So it had been a bit of a shock to her when Edith Marrowbone who although having only written two books, 'The Lost Cord' (The Battersea Strangler) and 'The Missing Link' (The Bristol Shipping Murders) , both of which had appeared on the 'best sellers', made such a reply to her question. She suddenly felt that she had been put down in some way. Nevertheless, she proffered her green leather bound autograph book and her lucky Parker pen and waited.

Edith took the pen and book with good grace and enquired 'to whom shall I dedicate it to?'

'Oh just your signature would be perfect if that is alright?' said the small woman.

Edith signed her name with a flourish. She was surprised to note that the Parker was filled with green ink, she had always prided herself on judging people and she definitely had not expected green ink.

'Oh thank you very much Edith'

'It's Miss Marrowbone' said Edith as she turned and swept away from the woman.

Edith had travelled down to Motley Hall three days ago. She planned to use the forthcoming safari expedition as research for a new book that she was working on. The new storyline was shaping up nicely. She just needed this extra research to hone some of the finer points.

Some writers Edith mused liked to go headlong into a story and see where it takes them. Others prefer to carefully craft the plot, the characters and perhaps two or three alternative endings and then join up the dots. Edith was really a mixture of the two. She liked to get a basic skeleton of the story in her mind and then she would fire away at one character and see how far she could go with their piece of the plot. She would then weave in another character and then another until the spider's web started to hang together.

Next came the bit that she really liked, adding in her research. Here she would add in the places and situations, the local customs, the quirky facts. It was these details that brought the whole thing together, brought it to life, changed it from just words on a page to a book that the reader couldn't put down until they had discovered and experienced every last twist and the story was finally revealed.

This Edith believed was the skill of an author. Someone once said that there is at least one good book in everyone. She didn't believe this for a moment, she believed that many people had the idea of a good book in them but being able to bring all of the elements together was a skill that blessedly for her was only given to a few.

She had been outside taking in the last of the fresh air when the autograph hunter had approached her. The weather looked as if it was about to make a turn for the worse. She drew her shawl a little tighter around her shoulders and welcomed the idea that tomorrow morning she would be on her way to somewhere far warmer. She gazed out across the front lawn and noticed a very dishevelled looking policeman wheeling, with some considerable difficulty, a sack truck of luggage along the driveway that led around the side of the main building. To say that she was surprised by his arrival would have been an understatement. He looked as though he had been in a hay barn. She smiled inwardly at this fine example of law of English law and order.

*

Edith had never been outgoing, she was basically a very insecure individual and this had manifested itself, to almost everyone she came into contact within her small world in North London, as shy. Edith knew it was much more than that. Her father was a very successful industrialist who spent the majority of Edith's formative years working abroad. She felt she hardly knew him because even during the times when her father was home, he worked such long hours in his study holding meetings that she hardly ever saw him.

He very often had guests who would arrive at the front door and be taken straight away in to his study. On very rare occasions, a guest would be asked to sit and wait in the morning room. They would be asked if they wished for some refreshment and would then wait until, Edith assumed, a point in the meeting had arrived or a discussion was completed that this person should not be privy to and then they would be asked, well really summoned, to join the meeting from that point onwards.

Sometimes, Edith would sit very quietly in the conservatory which adjoined the morning room and would watch these people completely unobserved from her position. Edith liked the power that she felt being able to watch someone who was clearly of some importance to her father and yet they did not know she even existed. Over a period of watching Edith began to identify a number of types and the one that she saw the most often was the nervous type.

They would decline the offer of refreshment and would sit very upright with their briefcase on their lap, knees very close together. Then as time went on they would check their watch, check their appearance, check the contents of the briefcase to make sure presumably that the papers they were going to talk about were still there. This checking for some was something of an obsession and they would check every few minutes and ruffle the papers, checking the order they were in and other such like repetitive mannerisms. Edith smiled to herself as she remembered one middle-aged gentleman with a bowler hat and funny little grey moustache. He had done the ritual of checking the papers in his briefcase just as many others did but then while checking them for the umpteenth time he was suddenly called in by the butler. The poor man almost jumped out of his skin and managed not only to drop all of the papers all over the floor but also the half-drunk cup of tea on to the papers to boot. Edith thought the poor man would die of a heart attack he looked so flustered!

Sometimes she would sneak along to the study doors and sit there listening to the conversations from within. She couldn't really hear anything in particular but she liked to listen to the changes in tone of the individuals who would be speaking. At times things were quite heated and voices became raised, sometimes it was her father who was speaking in a raised voice and sometimes it was another man though often when this happened her father would enter into the conversation and then it would all calm down again. She took this to mean that he was in charge and that he let people have their say but eventually he would bring them back into order.

Edith wondered for a long while how the meeting was conducted as the room had a large table with high back leather chairs along both sides and one larger chair positioned at the head where she guessed her father sat. But it also had a couple of large settees and armchairs that were grouped around.

She fancied in her thoughts that perhaps the business of the day was conducted around the table and then, when the discussions had been completed, the parties would retire to a more informal arrangement around the fireplace. She remembered how on one occasion while she was sitting on the carpet outside of the doors, Burrows the butler had returned to the room unexpectedly. She had been listening so intently to the noises coming from the room that she had not heard him coming along the carpeted corridor behind her.

'Excuse me Edith' he had whispered, making her nearly jump out of her skin, as he approached the doors. 'You know people who eavesdrop, rarely hear any good being said about them. You would do well to remember that.'

Edith often thought to herself that the servants should call her madam or miss but her mother had decided early on that the protocol in this household was that the children would be referred to by their Christian names until they reached adulthood as a mark of coming of age at twenty-one.

However, before she reached her coming of age, fate decided to intervene. Her father had been working in America and on the night flight back across the Atlantic during a wicked storm the plane 'developed problems in the engines' which had caused her father and fifty-five other poor souls to be lost in the biting cold water forever. The Ocean was over two miles deep and experts said it would be very unlikely if they ever found any wreckage at all and indeed they never did.

It all became too much for Edith's mother, she was never strong in her mind at the best of times and her decline first into depression, then drink and finally insanity was almost as sharp as the assumed trajectory of her father's aeroplane.

In less than two years she had effectively lost her parents and now after just turning nineteen years old, she found herself in the care of her Uncle Tristan and Aunt Elizabeth who lived in a large Victorian house in Epsom in Surrey. She had not had a great deal of contact with either her Aunt or Uncle over the years, just the odd family get together, perhaps a wedding or when either side of the family found themselves travelling so close to the other family member's home that it would have been considered rude not to visit. Edith thought they would probably be very strict but as it turned out they were quite the opposite, even bohemian in their outlook. They had only one child of their own, a boy five years Edith's junior who was very dull and would sit for hours in his room. She wasn't really sure what he got up to in there and she was never interested enough to find out.

Edith continued with her education at home until she was twenty years old and then Aunt Elizabeth arranged to embark on a female version of the Grand Tour of Europe which had been undertaken by young men for hundreds of years. Her Aunt knew her own child would never have the pluck to want to undertake such an adventure and so she decided that her niece would do it instead. Edith was naturally a little apprehensive at first but also very excited at the prospect of travelling to foreign countries for almost a year. She embraced the idea and joined her Aunt headlong in the preparations and she eagerly waited for the day when they would be off; their first stop would be Paris after all!

Now as a woman of twenty-eight, a successful published author and with plenty of money in her bank account, Edith Marrowbone reflected for one last moment on how that Grand Tour of Europe with her Aunt had changed her life. She had emerged from her cocoon of shyness and found that she was indeed a butterfly. She had discovered life, she had discovered men, and she had discovered passion.

Chapter Nine

Titus decided he had done enough socialising and made his way to his table. He noticed that to his right, the seat was occupied by a portly gentleman whom he knew owned an accountancy firm and was a major sponsor for this trip. Titus recalled that he had sat beside this gentleman before and apart from his bulk which made it difficult for anyone sitting adjacent to him to actually eat their meal in any sort of comfort, he was in fact surprisingly good company and so Titus resignedly settled down for what he hoped would be an enjoyable meal. He would worry about making his contact sometime later in the evening. For now it was time to listen to Lady Agatha doing what she did best….talk!

'Dear friends, it is wonderful to see you all gathered here and I have already had an opportunity to talk to a number of you individually but I thought it would be nice of me to formally welcome you to my traditional 'last night in England' farewell party before leaving these shores in the morning in search of adventure, discovery, excitement and who knows perhaps even treasure!'

An enthusiastic cheer went up from the guests followed by a short burst of clapping, led by Titus.

'Now, I have some important news. My assistant the Reverend Titus Jennings who I am sure you have all met and if you haven't you really need to speak to him as soon as you can as he makes the allocations for the berths, has confirmed with the shipping line that we will be actually now be leaving from Portsmouth.'

A general murmur went around the room.

'Yes I know that I have told many of you that we would be leaving from Southampton and I am sure that for those of you who are coming along to see us off, as well as a number of you who have friends and relatives coming on the day to do likewise, this news will be disappointing and that you will need to make alternative arrangements rather quickly. Trust me this is not something that is in my control and we have made a number of calls to make absolutely sure that Portsmouth is where we will embark and as I say that has been confirmed just now by Titus. And also remember ladies only one hat box will be allowed.'

Another rather more indignant and high pitched rumble could be heard around the room.

'One box is all that can be allowed because we don't have a great deal of capacity on the camel train when we arrive in Africa.'

Crispin Moorcock was on his feet in an instant, 'I say I didn't realise that we were going to have to travel by train with a bunch of camels. My father has paid good money for me to be on this trip and I would have expected that I would be afforded some level of luxury!'

Agatha turned slowly around to face Moorcock. 'Mr Moorcock. Firstly; a camel train is not a train that contains a number of the beasts, the train is made up entirely of camels which walk one after another across the desert. Secondly; everyone on this safari has paid the same fee and there are no differing levels of luxury for anyone and in your particular case your father has still not made a payment at all so unless we have confirmation of the funds wired to my account in the morning I fear that you will not be seeing the camel train at all!'

She returned to address the rest of the group once more.

'We will need to assemble in the hallway at six o-clock in the morning to board the charabanc that will be waiting to take us as swiftly as possible to Portsmouth. We are allowed to commence boarding our ship the S.S. Gloriana from six thirty tomorrow evening which should fit perfectly with our timetable. We sail on the morning tide at one fifteen and make our way along the coast of France, then across the Bay of Biscay passing Spain and then Portugal. We continue along by Gibraltar and then we stop at Algiers to pick up important tools and supplies that we will need on the expedition. We then sail on and arrive at Alexandria where we will disembark. The voyage should take us eight days. Once we disembark we will make our way by camel train directly to the site of the dig where we will get ourselves settled into camp. On the morning of the first day in camp we will take a short tour of the site as I am sure everyone will be very keen to learn the history of the area and the purpose of digging there.

Our whole trip will be six and half weeks returning to Southampton.'

But that is all ahead of us. For now, let us enjoy this wonderful dinner that my dear cousin has provided for us and then I suggest that we all get off to bed soon after so that we can all be bright eyed and with our tails as bushy as one can muster for six o-clock sharp. Thank you.'

A spontaneous ripple of applause (not led by Titus) echoed around the room as she moved down the stairs and took her seat at her table. She looked quickly around the room and her eyes settled on her target, 'Titus! Will you please say grace; so that we may begin?'

Titus was busily engaged in conversation with Mary-Belle who was voicing her concern about how she was expected to get all of her hats into one box. When the command came from Lady Agatha, he visibly jumped.

'Oh yes of course Lady Agatha. Forgive me Miss Devine; we will have to discuss your cabin requirements later.' He made his way to the steps. 'As most of us have now taken our places I would ask you to join me in The Grace.'

Titus suddenly saw an opportunity to broadcast his code word to everyone in one go. 'Before I do that however I was wondering has anyone ever been to Alsace Lorraine?' There was no reaction from anyone in the room with the exception of a steely look from Lady Agatha wondering what on earth was going on.

'Oh well, can we all bow our heads and say the grace, for what we are about to receive, may we all be truly thankful, Amen.'

The room resounded with a united 'Amen' and then conversations immediately started up and serving staff busied themselves serving bread and topping up the wine. Even though Burrows had tried very hard to conceal the whereabouts of the entrance to the wine cellar, he had completely misjudged Agatha's explorer's instinct. Once discovered and despite his protestations, she had wasted no time in showing him her extensive knowledge of wines picked up from many a night of drinking around the globe with a variety of wealthy and powerful men all of whom she had captivated with her charm. Thus she had selected all of best from the cellar for this evening's meal in ten minutes flat.

The wine was flowing and it was becoming apparent that for some, six in the morning was not going to be bright, bushy or even possible! Monty was becoming quite loud in his quest to entertain as many ladies as he could. He had not yet taken his seat and was standing with Mary-Belle Devine and as he reached for his glass Agatha moved over to him and grabbed it from the mantelpiece before he could take another swig. Unfortunately, Agatha's fingers were not quite as nimble as she would have liked and the glass dragged clumsily against the stone and the majority of the wine spilled on to the floor.

'I think that you have probably had quite sufficient now Monty. I don't want to have to be the one to report to your mother that you disgraced yourself by being so obviously 'in wine' that you didn't even make it on to the charabanc on the first morning.'

Monty appeared not to be listening to his Aunt and instead continued his conversation with Mary-Belle Devine who promptly stopped gazing at him when she heard the tone of Agatha Plantagenet's voice. Mary-Belle took Monty by the shoulder and turned him around so that he was facing in the direction of his Aunt. A servant arrived with a single glass of

Amaretto, Agatha's favourite tipple which she enjoyed with her evening meal with ritualistic monotony.

'I said I think you have probably had enough to drink Monty but I don't want to be seen as dull so here take this glass. I intended it for me but you may have it as my favourite nephew and let this be your very last drink. Agatha handed Monty the glass and moved away back to her table.

Monty took the glass and looked in the direction of Agatha. He knew that she was less than pleased with his antics but it wasn't as if this was the first time she had seen him like this. He had invited his Aunt on many occasions to the officer's mess parties and they had always been lively affairs to say the least. Little did she realise that he wasn't as drunk as he made out but he couldn't reveal that now. He had his own reasons.

He knew that Mary-Belle was looking at him and he turned to her and half winking, he raised his glass and drained the contents in one, in a gesture of defiance to his Aunt, who had walked away and was now seated with her back to him, so the gesture and the effort were completely lost on her though he noted that most of the room were looking in his direction. The sweet taste of the Amaretto clashed with the subtlety of the wine and it made him shudder for a moment. He decided he needed more wine to wash away this less than pleasant taste.

Monty turned once again to face Mary-Belle Devine who met his gaze with a smile. He began to open his mouth to ask her if she would like another drink but he was aware that his throat felt hot somehow as if he had just drunk some tea very quickly. He knew that Agatha's drink was not his usual but he was still surprised by the reaction he was feeling. He swallowed and tried to get rid of the sensation but instead the heat remained and was now joined by a similar sensation in his chest.

Mary-Belle stopped smiling and took a step forward towards him 'are you all right Monty? You're not looking at all well. Perhaps you should have a sit down over here' she indicated with her hand towards a nearby settee but Monty wasn't hearing her clearly any longer.

To him her voice appeared to be high pitched and accompanied with a hissing noise in his ears like escaping steam. His throat was now on fire and he was finding it increasingly difficult to breathe.

Mary-Belle shouted for help. Lady Agatha broke off her conversation and turned in her chair wondering what on earth all the commotion was about. She saw her nephew staggering towards her. He had both of his hands around his throat almost as if he was trying to strangle himself. He began ripping at his collar and his whole face was a brighter shade of red than his tunic.

Agatha rose from her seat and advanced towards him as he stumbled and crashed face down onto the flagstone floor. Mary-Belle screamed and covered her mouth with her hand looking on in disbelief at what was unfolding before her eyes. By the time Agatha had made the half dozen steps and arrived at Monty's side, her favourite nephew, her brave soldier, was already dead.

Chapter Ten

Bailey had been standing around while people took their seats for dinner. A servant came over to him and suggested that he might wish to take his seat as well. Bailey thought for a moment and then took the servant gently by the sleeve.

'The thing is I don't think that I am supposed to be dining with the guests. It's not what us Police usually do. We patrol see, we observe, we are good at that sort of thing.'

Though I am starving he thought to himself. He had eaten the sandwiches that Sarah had packed for him, sausage and pickle – his favourite, some hours before as he made his way along the road before the incident with the horse.

In fact he had trouble negotiating the sack truck at the same time as trying to eat and had, on more than one occasion, dropped the sandwich on the floor but with a quick dust off they were as good as new. He had also had some further sustenance from Rose's delightful cake but to his very active stomach that event was now a fading memory.

'There is a place set for you sir' the servant interrupted Bailey's thoughts with his comment. 'Oh well in that case I will come down to the kitchen as soon as I can' replied Bailey.

'Sir you misunderstand, you are on the seating plan. Look here I'll show you.'

The servant moved towards the large sheet of paper that was fixed to an artist's easel at the end of the room just in front of where Lady Agatha had made her address, and pointed to a name beautifully written in italics in strong black ink. 'PC Bailey' the name swirled along the line.

'My word so I am, well in that case young man lead on to where I am to be sitting down and enjoying this fine dinner without any further delay.'

The servant indicated to Bailey where he was to sit. 'Would you care to sit now sir?' The servant pulled out the chair and then slid it perfectly into position as Bailey sat while expertly reaching over in the same movement and snapped out the napkin and placed it into the constable's lap. Bailey took in his surroundings and then on noticing that the servant was now gliding away supposedly on his next task, he called after him.

'Excuse me but could you bring me another napkin please?' The servant half turned to Bailey and nodded that he had taken in the instruction, he then continued on his way to the kitchen.

Bailey sat and smiled and thought to himself 'well this is nice isn't it? I didn't expect to be eating up here with all the posh people. We don't get to dine quite so fine back at the station in Heavitree....in fact we don't have tablecloths at all!'

Bailey looked around at all the people who were still happily chatting with their glasses in their hands. Some were deep in conversations leaning in to each other, almost conspiratorially, while others stood apart and leaned theatrically backwards at the punchline to a joke. Others stood on the edge of a group of people just listening or perhaps standing awkwardly trying to fit in to the conversations. Bailey for his part was happy to be sitting after the walk from the station and he also liked to get seated early, this a throwback to dinner time in the station when sometimes there wasn't quite enough to go around and then being seated early was a real advantage. An older man of perhaps seventy came and took the seat next to him. He explained that he was a minor sponsor of the expedition and planned to join the party as far as Africa and then sail back on the returning tide, 'I suppose you all dine in a canteen sort of arrangement back at the station officer, this must be quite a treat?'

'Indeed it is Sir; we don't usually see so much silverware either except when we are laying out the haul from a burglary. A knife, fork and spoon are all we get and that's because it's usually sausages and potatoes, and the pudding is always something with custard. Mind you I'm not complaining, Helen, that's the cook, she does a really proper job with the grub'.

The servant returned with a fresh napkin as Bailey had requested. He deftly made to take away, what he assumed, was the offending napkin from Bailey's lap. Quick as a flash Bailey grabbed the servant's hand.

'Oh no, I don't want you to take this one. It is perfectly fine.'

'But I thought you said you wanted another sir?'

Bailey pulled the servant closer to his face so that he could talk into the man's ear. 'No I wanted a second one because we have soup coming and I have a uniform on'.

The servant was released from Bailey's grip and stood up looking puzzled. Bailey took the napkin and thanked the servant before he unfolded it and tucked it with some effort, as the high collar on a policeman's uniform does not leave much room for additional accoutrements, into the top of his collar. 'Perfect' said Bailey not to anyone in particular.

He now sat completely bedecked in fresh white linen and awaited the arrival of the soup, happy in the thought that he was now prepared. The servant, satisfied that his job here was done, moved away to other duties.

Lost in his own thoughts, he wasn't immediately aware of the commotion to the left of him. People were still milling around and chatting quite loudly and at first he didn't notice that some of them were now looking at him. 'Bailey!' He could hear a voice but couldn't place who it was or exactly where it was coming from; the acoustics in this large room with such a high ceiling was very confusing. He had noticed this when Lady Agatha had made her speech earlier. 'Bailey! Where the devil are you? Come quickly!' He looked up and noticed that now everyone around him was staring straight at him. The old gentleman had half risen from his seat and was indicating to him to stand as well. 'Bailey!' it was then that he realised who owned that voice, it was the same one that had echoed off the ceiling earlier, it was Agatha. He stood up and looked around him.

'You are wanted man, over there' the old man was staring him in the face.

'Oh right then'. Bailey moved away from the table to the other side of the room and was confronted with the scene of Lady Agatha with a face that looked like it might explode kneeling next to the figure of Major Montague Fortescue-Smythe lying face down on the floor. Mary-Belle Devine was being attended to by a couple of waiting staff on a settee that was close by. She appeared to have fainted.

'Bailey, where the devil have you been!?' thundered Agatha 'you are supposed to be here doing crowd control!'

'I am Madam but I wasn't aware..'

'Don't argue! Can't you see I need your help here? Monty has collapsed.'

Bailey moved nearer the body and with help from one of the servants and with Agatha overseeing the operation, the Major was turned over to reveal a face with the ghastliest expression of pain written across it. The corners of his mouth were drawn upwards exposing his front teeth in a garish smile while his dead eyes bulged hideously. His whole countenance was a reddish purple.

Mary-Belle took one look at his face, screamed and once again fell in a dead faint.

Bailey, still wearing his napkin around his neck, quickly placed it over the unfortunate Major's face and organised a few of the servants to help carry the body into the study and had him laid out on the large desk.

Bailey left the room for a short while and when he returned Lady Agatha was almost the only person left. The last stragglers who had come to look at what was going on were leaving, some with a backward glance to the sight of the body lying silently on the desk while some just hugged each other and hurriedly moved back into the main room with their heads down wanting to erase the image from their mind.

Agatha had drawn up a chair near to the side of her nephew and she held his hand up against her cheek. 'You know Bailey; he really was a lovely boy. He was brash, he drank too much and he chased women but to me he was always just Monty, there was never any pretence when he spoke to me. I will miss him and how I will break this news to his poor mother goodness knows. It will destroy her.

I know we are going to arrange the post mortem as soon as we can but I fear it will only show what I already know and that is as I say, that he drank far too much and far too often.'

'Yes that may well be the case Lady Agatha but I have made some arrangements which could be good news on the post mortem front if it all works out. If it does, then I will share it with everyone as I am convinced they will be pleased to know that things are moving on so quickly. It isn't good for anyone, especially those going such a long way away to have this sort of thing happen just the night before the journey and no explanation.'

I need to help with the preparations Lady Agatha so perhaps it would be better if you were to leave this to me now.

Lady Agatha continued to hold his hand against her face 'you know, he is still warm, it's just as if he, he..' she broke off and Bailey knew that he was witnessing a side of Lady Agatha Plantagenet that few people probably ever saw. She was in fact human and frail just like the rest of us.

Bailey touched her arm and she slowly looked up and nodded in agreement. 'Yes Bailey, you must do what you can, as soon as you can.'

She placed Monty's arm gently down by his side and then rose from the chair. She searched in her handbag and found a large handkerchief. She dabbed at her eyes and then blew her nose with a loud hoot that sounded out of place in the silence of the room. He led Agatha from the room and closed the door softly. He thought about the task in hand and knew that he didn't really know what to do from here but he considered what the sergeant would have done and then he recalled the conversations that he had heard in the canteen from the other blokes. He remembered that above all else he must not be swayed by what Agatha had said and how she had behaved because that was often something that guilty people did to throw you off the scent. He also recalled that it was always a good idea to check the pockets of the deceased before anyone else got a chance and so he began his search.

The noise outside of the door had started to rise again and so Bailey relaxed a little knowing that some normality was returning to the dining room which was a good thing. Sudden deaths, he thought to himself, were always a disturbing thing and could really ruin a party.

The trouser pockets had not turned up anything at all and he was coming to the conclusion that this was going to be just the unfortunate death of a man who had simply drunk himself to death when, on searching the small ticket pocket to the right side of Monty's tunic jacket, he discovered a piece of paper that had been deliberately folded up very small. He took it out and unfolded it very carefully. The lighting in this room was fairly subdued so he moved away from the body until he was directly under the lamp and then began to examine what he had discovered.

The note read as follows;
The Officers Racing Club, 41 Whitehall, London, England

: Message Begins: 0630 am 1st August 1937
  M. Fortescue Smythe. (Falcon)
Information confirmed concerning presence of German High Command Advisor who has infiltrated safari party and will leave England with them on next trip. Identity of advisor unknown, more information to follow. Proceed with all caution. Precise mission of advisor unknown, possible links with military installations or smuggling.
: Message Ends: Acknowledge received.

Bailey thought for a minute. He didn't know why but the name of the club rang a bell with him. It was something that his sergeant had said to him. He was always reading information about lots of things and from time to time when he didn't have anything else to do he used to sit Bailey down and try, as he saw it, to 'put some knowledge in the Constable's head'.

While Bailey continued to ponder what it was that he knew about this club he set the paper down on a small occasional table with a red leather inlay which had been exquisitely engraved in intricate gold flowers. The pattern reminded Bailey of something he had seen in a book about China. He wondered if indeed the table itself had come from there.

The far door opened and a large recognisable shape all dressed in white appeared and said 'Oh John there you are, I got the message that you wanted to see me about something' in that same voice so soft that it seemed incongruous with his large bulk.

Bailey looked up from his deliberations about the note 'oh Charles it's you. Please come in, I have an idea that you might be able to help me out here. I remembered what you told me about your previous profession and I wondered if you might be able to give the Major a quick once over and tell us what happened to him'.

'As I said, I used to be a vet so I might be able to give you some indication though it is all a bit irregular. Are you sure that you have the authority to ask me to do this John?'

'Oh yes I would have thought it would be fine. The point is I have just tried the telephone and it appears not to be working. That butler chap Burrows tells me this happens quite a lot here so I will try again later but in the meantime that means I've no idea where I might be able to find anyone medical that can take a look at the body and I think it's important from my point of view as being in charge of crowd control and looking after famous people like Lady Agatha for instance, that I find out exactly what did happen to the unfortunate Major Monty as soon as possible. As you know the party are off in the morning and who knows you might discover that there's something seriously wrong with him and I'll need to tell everyone else.'

The big man looked at Bailey for a second and then over to the silent body of Monty before returning his gaze to Bailey 'well yes I am pretty certain already that there is something seriously wrong with the Major. I am fairly certain that he is dead.'

Bailey clapped his hands to the side of his head 'oh yes I already know that though it's always good to get it from a medical person, even if it is an animal medical person. No what I actually meant was that perhaps he has died of some serious contagious illness and if that is the case then it is certainly something that we will be wanting to tell everyone else about before they start off on their safari, wouldn't you agree? Anyway, we need to move the body downstairs so that you can have a look at him in some better light?'

Crawford moved past Bailey to Monty. 'I have a number of kitchen porters coming around with a handcart. We will take him to the outhouse behind the kitchen and I'll see what I can find out but you must understand Constable that I am not really qualified or used to this sort of thing with human bodies and so it will only be a very brief examination.'

Bailey waved his hand dismissively and made to leave the room happy that everything was taken care of as far as Monty was concerned. On reaching the door he turned to Crawford 'I don't suppose for a minute that the Officers Racing Club in Whitehall in London means anything at all to you does it?'

Crawford looked puzzled and shook his head. Bailey already knew that would be the answer because he had remembered what his sergeant had said and that was now bothering him. He needed to find Lady Agatha, at the end of the day he was here to do crowd control and it was her crowd that he was controlling so it made sense to him that she should be the person that he gave this information to. On his way back out into the dining room it occurred to him that perhaps it would be more helpful if he just asked everyone at the same time. After all he still had to give them all the good news about Monty and Lady Agatha would be just as much a suspect if Crawford had discovered anything out of the ordinary.

Chapter Eleven

He quickly made his way across the room and climbed the stairs. On reaching the landing he turned to face his audience. 'Ladies and gentlemen, I have some good and bad news about Mr Monty that I thought you would like me to share with you. On top of that I also have found out some information which I need to tell you with the hope that you might be able to help me. So the first thing to say is the bad news that Major Monty Fortescue Smythe is definitely dead.'

From around the room there was a mixture of tutts of indignation that this fool of a Policeman could make such an obvious statement while from others there were little shrieks of shock and the odd sharp intake of breath. Bailey also fancied that he heard the mumblings of a male voice saying that it wasn't very surprising given the amount the Major was known to drink.

Bailey continued 'The good news however is that we are able to carry out a preliminary post mortem here as Chef Crawford used to be a vet and as soon as we know anything I will let you know.'

This time the noise in the room was more a universal gasp with the realisation that the man preparing their food was also going to be preparing Monty.

Bailey thought twice about slipping in that 'perhaps it would be a good idea to avoid the dark meat course' in an effort to lighten the mood but at the last moment he thankfully decided that it might not go down well with some of the guests and Monty's Aunt was in the room after all. So instead he decided to move on to read out the note that he had found on the body.

As he began to read it out Bailey became aware of just how silent the room had become, the people seemed to be almost straining to hear every syllable that he uttered. He fancied that it was the fascination that people have with dead bodies but he also wondered if it was because he the Policeman had asked them for his help. On finishing the note Bailey looked out at the upturned faces and added the final twist that he had recalled from his conversations with his sergeant.

'The odd thing is ladies and gentlemen, there isn't an Officers Racing Club, at that address in Whitehall. The reason I know this is because my desk sergeant studies things to do with spies and intrigue, it is something that has always fascinated him and this note would have him jumping off his stool. You see that address is actually the address of the British Secret Service.'

Another collective gasp around the room.

'Yes, you may well gasp. The question we therefore have to ask is does this letter have the wrong address on it? To me that appears very unlikely as this is printed staticnery. If that is not the case, then it seems that Major Montague Fortescue-Smythe may well have been a successful officer in the army but it also appears to be true that he was also a spy.'

Yet another, bigger, gasp of amazement from the guests.

'So the next question is, ladies and gentlemen, was Monty here spying on his Aunt or was he spying on someone else or was he not spying at all. If he wasn't spying then why did he have a note about spying on him or was the note given to him perhaps by a spy. Or was he in fact just here on holiday?'

The faces around the room reflected a single thought at this last utterance from the Police Constable, a thought that many had made before and undoubtedly would do again. 'How on Earth has this man lasted so long in the Police Force?'

With that Bailey put away the note and made his way back to his table just in time to see the soup being served. It was good to note that a little thing like the death of one of the guests had not put the serving staff off their stroke and from the fact that people had taken their seats at the table, it clearly hadn't affected anyone's appetite very much either.

Bailey carefully repositioned his napkins and took his seat. He was slightly concerned when he peered down into the soup to find small pieces of bread floating in his bowl. He wondered if the servant had done it on purpose because he had asked for another napkin but when he noticed that everyone else appeared to have some too, he tried it and found it to be delicious. He made a note to mention to Crawford just how good the soup was though he guessed he was probably busy just at the moment.

Chapter Twelve

Titus returned to the table somewhat shocked at the turn of events and helped a young lady to take her seat which was opposite his. She told him she was from Caerphilly in South Wales. She was travelling with her new husband and they were joining this expedition as part of their honeymoon. They would remain on the ship once the main party had been put ashore. She was very excited about the whole prospect.

Titus was fairly sure that this couldn't be his contact and so relaxed a little.

He knew that he needed to use the code word that he had been given in order to be able to locate his contact. He casually checked the menu while he waited for his food to be served. He had not been seated for more than a minute when he smelt the intoxicating smell of expensive perfume. He was aware that someone had taken the seat immediately to his left but before he could register who it was, there came the edgy tones of a well-educated voice 'I suppose this is all a bit old hat to you. After all this is not your first trip abroad is it and I wouldn't have thought it was your first dead body either?'

Titus turned to face the woman. 'Ah Miss Marrowbone, I wondered when we would meet. I have been one of your readers for a while. In answer to your first question, yes I have been abroad a number of times with Lady Agatha but you are wrong to think that I think of this as 'old hat'. I am always very excited about the prospect of travel but it does create an awful lot of work to make sure that things run smoothly. Agatha is such a stickler on everything you know. Talking of which, I am not entirely sure if you are sitting in the right seat. On the other hand, perhaps it is me that has made the mistake. I will need to go and consult the table plan once again. Lady Agatha will work herself into a real tizzy if people are not seated where she has instructed or perhaps I should say 'suggested' that they should sit. With regard to dead bodies; I have officiated at funerals of course but the bodies were all in boxes if you understand my meaning. It is really quite dreadful about the poor Major. Did you know him at all?'

'Indeed Reverend Jennings. It is quite awful. I did have a very brief conversation with him earlier during drinks. I can hardly believe that in such a short time he is now no longer with us.'

She paused for a moment before continuing.

'Of course you believe he has now gone to a better place and that must give you a lot of comfort and it is that belief that allows you to minister such peace and comforting words to those of us that do not have the conviction that you do in your faith. I find it admirable, that drive, that…passion. You also surprise me Reverend Jennings, I would never have thought that you would be a reader of my novels but then I am constantly amazed at my audience. I have never really tried to appeal to a particular group of people and so it is always a surprise to find out just who is reading my work.

I write purely for myself in the first instance and then my publisher sends my work out into the wide world and I sit back and wait to see the reaction of my readers. Up until now I am very pleased to say my stories have always been met favourably by the public at large. Now please let me know if I have misread the seating plan. I wouldn't want to start off this trip on the wrong side of anyone and certainly not Lady Agatha. In a way I feel that I am on this trip under false pretences because I do not really have any interest in being part of a safari. For me it is all about the research so I really want to keep my head below the parapet so to speak.'

'Yes fully understandable Miss Marrowbone, given where we are going and the current state of affairs. My faith does indeed give me the inner strength dear lady and with that strength I can continue even in the face of death itself'. Regarding your stories, they are so well written Miss Marrowbone that it is easy to understand why they are so popular. I particularly liked your last novel 'The lost cord' you know, about the strangler. It was really gripping, if, if you will pardon the pun of course. It kept me guessing right up until the end, really marvellous stuff. And what about the fact that the Major turns out to be a spy of some sort or other, surely there is the making for another novel right here?'

Edith warmed to the compliment, 'Thank you Reverend Jennings for your kind words. I do not like to make such light comment of the untimely demise of the Major but suffice it to say, I have already made some notes!'

'Oh please, let's dispense with the Reverend shall we, please call me Titus.'

'Alright then, Titus, I will do just that but you in return must call me Edith. You say that you have travelled a lot with Lady Agatha. Would you mind telling me where? As I have already alluded to the main purpose of my coming on this safari in the first place, is to do some research on Africa and in particular Egypt for my new book.'

A thought suddenly came to Titus that although he was sure this charming lady could not be his contact; this was an ideal opportunity to repeat the code word in a conversation and yet make it seem as if everything was normal.

'Um I was wondering Miss Marrowbone that in the research that you must have carried out for your previous novels whether you ever had an occasion to travel to Europe and perhaps even to, to, to Alsace Lorraine for instance?'

Titus blurted out the code word and was already cursing himself under his breath that he had got so nervous right at the end. If this was his contact they would be thinking what a fool he was at this point, though in truth he had gone off the whole idea of meeting up with a contact and also with going through with the whole pictures thing anymore in any case.

'I have been to Europe on many occasions Titus but I cannot recall this place that you speak of. I noted that you mentioned it just before you said Grace. Does it have some significance for you?

Titus breathed a sigh of relief that his poor performance at trying to make his contact speech had actually worked even though he had stumbled so badly over the words. 'No, no Miss Marrowbone I was just curious. It has been very nice to meet you but before I can remain in my seat I must just go and speak to Lady Agatha for a moment.'

'Yes of course dear man. You must do what you must do. However when you have a moment, we must talk. I understand you are allocating cabins and I must see what you have in mind for me.'

He rose and nodding to Edith and the other people who were also seated at the table, he made his excuses and moved away in the general direction of where he knew Lady Agatha would be.

He failed to see Lady Agatha and so returned to his seat and noted that Edith Marrowbone was no longer to his left. The seat had been taken by a much older woman who smelt faintly of horses. He tried very hard not to wrinkle his nose as he looked in her direction and gave a polite smile. He unfurled his freshly starched napkin into his lap. Something flashed past in his peripheral vision and landed under the table. At first he thought it was nothing more than a piece of the napkin but when he drew his chair back and bent down to pick it up he realised that it was a neatly folded piece of paper.

He picked it up, returned to his seat and opened it. It was a note which read as follows;

Titus,

I know that it is not easy to make our transaction without arousing suspicion. However, the deal must be done tonight and so I will give you our sign after the main course and expect you to follow at close distance.

I will be able to give you your final reward at this time. Do not become alarmed, remain as calm as possible it will all work out for our mutual benefit.

Titus quickly sat up straight and looked around him. He couldn't see anyone looking at him in particular. Who had put the paper there; could it have been Edith Marrowbone? Had anyone else passed his seat while he was away? Was it in the napkin or under the napkin? He wasn't sure. The note said that he would be given a sign but he didn't have a clue what the sign would be. This was clearly his contact but he must remain calm as instructed even though his heart was racing and he was sure that the people sat beside him must hear it beating because he could hear it pounding in his own ears. He thought it just might burst!

He was already a bundle of nerves what with the pressure of sorting out this trip as well as being at the constant beck and call of Lady Agatha and now with this terrible death of the Major right in front of everyone, it was all too much. Titus considered that he should just ignore the note; pretend in fact that he hadn't seen it at all. But he knew that the consequences of not handing over what he had learned from his last trip to Casablanca would be severe. He knew he was in far too deep now to back out but he also knew that his agenda had changed and he was in the driving seat here.

He decided not to rush and be obvious so he waited until he had finished his main course and then calmly made his excuses to his fellow diners that he needed to check some information for the voyage tomorrow. He slipped away from the Great Hall and went up the servant's staircase to the first floor. He still had no idea what the sign would be but he felt sure that he hadn't received it as yet. He decided that he would collect the information from his room and then wait around near the entrance door downstairs. He felt better that this way he was somehow in control of the situation and his confidence was slowly returning the more he reminded himself. In fact, after a while he was feeling so much better that he decided he could go through with the transaction. However, he decided that the amount of effort he had put in to gain this information was worth far more than the paltry sum that was being offered. He was going to ask for more, he was going to ask for double in fact and if his contact, whoever it might turn out to be, didn't like it then they would have to live with the disappointment.

Titus reached his room and after taking a quick look around to make sure that he had not been followed, he went inside. The room was dark, he had left the window open and the stirrings of the storm strengthened the wind which made the curtains billow softly into the room like sails on an ancient galleon.

He crossed to the window and closed it. He drew the curtains and then switched on the small bedside lamp. Moving to the bottom of his bed he lifted up the corner of the mattress and took out the small flat package wrapped in brown waxed paper. He unwrapped it carefully and checked the contents. He liked the feel of the wax paper, so precise in its folds, he knew everything would be there, he had checked the contents of this package so many times but he still wanted to be sure; no slip ups at this stage of the game.

Everything was there, he had excelled himself really. The people who wanted this information had no idea just how thorough he had been, how successful he had been, how devious....who would have thought it of a vicar?

He stood up from the end of the bed and opened the door leading back out to the corridor. He could hear the sounds from the Great Hall below him. He held the package in his hand, halfway out of the door he glanced back towards the bedside lamp and considered whether he should turn it off. Suddenly he felt a force pushing him back inside his room, he was taken unawares and he caught his foot under the edge of the rug and went sprawling across the floor. In an effort to check his fall he spread out his hands and the contents of his carefully wrapped package scattered in all directions.

'So Titus what have we here?' the voice was almost a whisper but very calm. 'My note was clear that I would give you a signal and yet I noticed you leave. Now what could be the reason for that I wondered? Then I thought well he probably isn't carrying the package with him right now so he will have to go and fetch it. So that made me think rather than give you a signal why don't I just follow you and then we can make the transaction in private?'

'I never imagined for a minute that it would be you.'

'You see there's the beauty of the whole thing Titus, the point of being undercover is that you are the one that is least suspected. Isn't that obvious when you think about it? Hidden in plain sight, that's the trick'

Titus attempted to regain his composure and stood up. 'I have been thinking about the deal.'

'Oh really Titus. And let me guess you think that you need to renegotiate the terms is that it?' The voice remained calm but now was laced with menace. 'Ah, just looking at your face tells me that I have read the situation perfectly. You know that I am not authorised to negotiate. Everything has already been agreed. However, I told you in my note that I would give you your final reward and I promise you I won't disappoint.'

Titus looked directly into the face that was confronting him and didn't recognise what those cold eyes were telling him until it was far too late to do anything to prevent it.

There was no pain; it was surprising really he had always thought that such an action would cause great agony. What he was surprised about was the swiftness and the sheer strength behind the thrust. He almost admired it oddly.

He coughed and realised his throat was filling with something warm, he knew it was his own blood and now it was filling his mouth until he couldn't hold it in any longer and it poured through his teeth and down the front of his cassock like a dark, silent waterfall.

The killer gently pushed away from Titus Jennings drawing the stiletto knife back out of his chest. Titus had mercifully lost consciousness even before his body toppled backwards hitting his head on the floor with a sickening crack.

Chapter Thirteen

'Titus are you there?' a woman's voice called out in the corridor. 'Titus' the voice called again but this time almost outside of the door. A number of the guests on the tables closest to the edge of the room directly below where Titus Jennings's bedroom was located heard the second cry and looked up in the general direction of the sound. The scream that came next stopped almost everyone in the room from whatever they were doing and they heard a woman's voice very clearly. 'Oh my God, he's been murdered! The Reverend has been murdered! Please someone come and help him!'

A head appeared over the side of the gallery it was the face of Mary-Belle Devine. Her beautiful face now looked contorted, terrified even, she was shouting again but now her voice was drowned by the commotion that was building below in the Great Hall. Some people jumped up out of their seats and began running for the stairs while others stood pointing in the direction of Mary-Belle.

Lady Agatha who had just returned to her seat after trying unsuccessfully to telephone her friend Inspector Lansdowne, cast her gaze around the room then, stood up from her table and marched with great determination over to where PC Bailey was still eating, apparently oblivious to the commotion around him, and bellowed 'Bailey, you are supposed to be in charge of controlling the crowd and looking around me at the chaos, I think you are doing a pretty poor job. What is more concerning however is that you seem to have not even noticed that there is a young woman screaming 'murder' at the top of her voice from the minstrel's gallery above and you have as yet to rise from your seat. I wonder PC Bailey if you would be good enough to join the rest of the concerned folk around here and kindly direct yourself to the first floor via that staircase located behind you and perhaps provide some assistance to the unfortunate woman. That is if it is not going to be too much trouble!!!'

'Actually Lady Agatha, I had noticed what was going on and was already in the act of getting myself away from the table and off to see what was going on. The only reason why you find me still here is because I was just about to ask if anyone else on the table knew where the staircase was. As you can see I am sitting with my back to it and hadn't noticed it. Now that you have kindly pointed it out, I will be on my way without further delay.'

Bailey was out of his seat and weaving around Agatha who remained directly behind him, her hands firmly planted on her hips and clearly unimpressed with him, he bounded up the stairs. Reaching the first floor he followed the people already hurrying along the main length of the gallery to the far side where a small crowd had gathered outside of one of the bedrooms. On arriving he pushed his way as politely as possible through the group blocking the doorway and entered the room where he saw the body of Titus Jennings lying sprawled on his back. From his mouth there led a thick shiny trail of blood down his chin and around his neck and into a dark pool that was forming from his shoulder to his hip. Bailey had rarely seen so much blood. Suddenly he became aware of all the people that were pushing and shoving to try and get a look at what had gone on. He heard a woman scream and he knew he had to move them all away from the bedroom door.

'All right everybody I think we have all seen enough. Let us try and give the man some respect shall we? That's it, let's move out of the room and back onto the landing. I would suggest that we all go back downstairs as I am sure it will be time for the puddings any moment now and you won't want to miss that now will you?'

The people being bundled out of the bedroom gave Bailey a quizzical look at his comments but then most people looked like that at Bailey and it didn't really make any difference to him.

Lady Agatha arrived.

'Bailey this is the second time in the same evening that I find myself in a room with you and a dead body. On the first occasion it was my dear nephew Monty whose cause of death is uncertain and now I find that my assistant dear Titus lies here on the floor of his room and he has clearly been murdered. The question that leaps into my mind Bailey is you are clearly out of your depth and I would suggest that you contact the local Police station and they in turn contact people who know what they are doing.'

This statement from Lady Agatha was followed by a loud rumble of thunder. For an instant Bailey thought it had been generated by the formidable woman herself which wouldn't have surprised him. He realised however that it was the storm heralding its approach. Bailey stood motionless taking in the situation and the comments that Agatha had made. It was pretty clear to him that things at this precise moment were not going well. He recounted the words from his desk sergeant this morning "So think carefully, think twice....no make that three times, about any actions you might want to take before you take them, always be near a telephone so that you can ask someone, anyone, if you need to make any decision other than which sandwich to eat next, don't lose any of the guests and generally and above all else just don't muck it up. All right?"

He was already thinking that one suspicious death and one murder did not sit well with these simple instructions. His face brightened for a moment when he thought that at least he had not technically 'lost' any of the guests because he knew exactly where they all were, it's just that a couple of them were dead but he thought this might not be exactly what the Sergeant meant.

'Lady Agatha I do understand what you're saying but the thing is there is no one at all at the local station as they have all gone out on the skittles evening. I am the only Policeman in the vicinity and so I will just have to do the best I can.'

'You are incompetent Bailey.'

'Actually I am Church of England Lady Agatha but I don't see that is going to help much at the moment.'

Agatha turned in despair from the Policeman and moved over to the scene that confronted her in the middle of the room. Agatha could feel the revulsion rise in her body as she stared into the once cheerful eyes of Titus Jennings as he lay sprawled across the floor. It was then that she took her first real look at the papers that lay about the body. Some had landed on the floor close to the body and were now bound in the pool of sticky red blood that was already congealing by the right side of the body. She avoided touching these and tried to only breathe out during her brief examination of the pictures so that she could avoid the distinctive, almost metallic smell of the blood.

'I recognise these pictures Constable' Agatha motioned Bailey to join her as she gathered up further pictures from the floor where they had been flung across the bedroom. 'Yes there is no doubt in my mind PC Bailey, these pictures are of the military installations near Casablanca. I managed to arrange it with some of the boys on the base for Titus to go up in an aeroplane and they photographed a number of installations in the vicinity and the base itself. But why on earth are they here? These photographs were in my possession only this morning. I plan to use them for research for a book that I am going to write. Titus must have removed them from my room unless of course it was his murderer and they threw them over the body. But why would they do that?'

'The motive of the murderer is often something that can be very difficult to work out your Ladyship'

82

'Yes Bailey, I am sure that is the case but if you really are the only Policeman available to work on this case, which is less than satisfactory, then you must use your previous experience of murders to work it out and quickly!'

Bailey nodded and kept his own counsel, he wasn't about to let on to her that he had in fact never worked on a murder enquiry in his life and that his quote came from something he had once read in a threepenny crime novel.

'Oh poor Titus, why would anyone want to hurt such a gentle man?' Agatha was mopping her eyes with a handkerchief for a second time this evening.

'Now nothing is to be gained by you getting upset Lady Agatha. I suggest you re-join your guests and I will arrange with the staff to help with Mr Jennings here.' Bailey crossed over to Lady Agatha who had perched herself on the edge of the bed and gently placed his hands on her shoulders. She slowly rose from her position and he guided her to the doorway.

'Bailey you realise what has happened here changes everything tonight? Titus was clearly murdered which means that unless the murderer has escaped then they are still here in amongst the rest of us. You must use every skill that you have in order to keep the good people safe and to bring this person or perhaps persons to book as soon as possible. It must be resolved before we leave in the morning Bailey otherwise we may well be taking a murderer with us to foreign shores.'

The fact that the murderer may have left the premises had not occurred to Bailey straight away but now that Agatha had pointed it out he realised that was definitely a possibility. A couple of kitchen porters arrived at the door and Bailey ushered them in and told them what he wanted them to do. The men hardly seemed to notice the blood and merely took the hands and feet of the little vicar and hauled him up on to the bed. It occurred to Bailey as he watched them that, to them, moving this body was no different to moving a side of pork. He had already picked up the remaining photographs from off the floor and had put them on one side so that he could study them again later but as they moved the body a couple more pictures were revealed. He quickly snatched them up and stored them with the others. The shortest of the porters stopped in front of Bailey on his way out 'Chef said he would like to have a word if you have a moment Constable. He's down in the kitchen.'

On his way back from the kitchen where he found Crawford overseeing a wonderful pudding sauce, he realised he was going to have to take control of things here. He knew he was out of his depth but he also knew that there wouldn't be any help coming any time soon. Crawford had also told him of his initial observations on what had killed Monty and what he had said was going to make things much worse.

He had tried to call the police station but as he had already suspected there wasn't anyone there. This sort of thing doesn't happen in sleepy little villages which is why they can close up shop and go off and play skittles for the night without any worries. Bailey replaced the receiver and thought about what his next move should be. The desk at Exeter would be manned that's for sure and so as much as he knew it was going to bring down all sorts of recriminations for himself, he knew that he must phone his desk sergeant and get help. He picked up the phone for a second time but this time there was no answer. He wiggled the contact arm but still nothing, another boom of thunder came from overhead and Bailey wondered if the line had become a victim of the weather. The storm had really picked up and the rain lashed against the windows.

He thought about sending someone from the Hall to make contact with the skittle team but then when he was on the point of selecting someone it occurred to him that if the murderer had not left the building then how could he be sure that the person he was sending was not the murderer and that he would be giving them the perfect escape route?

As soon as Bailey stepped back into the Great Hall all conversations stopped and every face turned to him as one.

'Ladies and Gentlemen, I apologise for having had to leave you for a while but I am sure you understand I had to make arrangements for Reverend Jennings.' More thunder boomed, as if the elements had decided to provide a dramatic underscore to everything he had to say. 'The fact is we find ourselves with a very difficult situation and I am not really sure where to begin.'

'Well just begin somewhere man, there is clearly a murderer in our midst if they haven't already escaped and you don't appear to have done anything at all to apprehend them!' Crispin Moorcock had risen from his seat and stood with his arms outstretched like a shepherd moving his flock forwards. From the half muttered comments from others around the room that followed his statement it was clear to Bailey that he had support for his point of view.

'Thank you Mr Meercroft.'

'It's Moorcock Bailey not Meercroft. Moor – cock, big M...small C got it?'

'Yes thank you Mr er Moorcock. The reason why I am unsure where to begin is because I have more information than you are aware of and I am still trying to make sense of it myself. However, I'll crack on and tell you how I see the situation and we can all go from there. Earlier this evening many of you witnessed the Major becoming unwell and falling to the floor over there' Bailey indicated with his arm to the spot where the unfortunate Major Montague Fortescue-Smythe had finally come to rest. 'Well as I said to you earlier we were fortunate that the Mr Crawford the Chef was able to carry out a preliminary examination of his body and he is convinced that the Major was in fact poisoned.'

A wave of gasps echoed around the room as well as more than one or two cries of 'what!'

Lady Agatha advanced towards him 'PC Bailey, are you trying to tell us that my Nephew's death was not an occupational accident but that he was also murdered supposedly by the same person or persons that so cruelly murdered poor Titus?'

'Unfortunately Lady Agatha that is exactly what I am telling you. The Chef is convinced that Prussic Acid otherwise known as Cyanide was the poison used. There were plenty of classic symptoms of poisoning and there is a very strong smell of almonds around his mouth.'

'Well the smell of the almonds would have been from my drink which was Amaretto. It is a liqueur made from almonds. I passed it to him and told him to make this his last drink.'

'And indeed it was his last drink wasn't it Lady Agatha?'

'PC Bailey, what exactly are you suggesting?'

'Oh nothing at all. I was merely stating that it was his last drink, meaning he didn't drink anything else after it. But I see what you mean; you think I said that you gave him the drink that poisoned him as if you are the poisoner. Oh dear that complicates things even further than I had thought we were at. Oh dear this really isn't good at all. Because the fact is you did give him the drink that poisoned him. But if we are to believe that it wasn't you that poisoned him and at this stage that is not yet decided, we will also have to consider that if you didn't poison him then the drink wasn't meant for him at all. It was meant for you Lady Agatha!'

More gasps from around the room. Lady Agatha clutched her throat as if suddenly finding it difficult to breathe. She was helped back to her seat by a servant standing nearby. She gratefully took the seat and a balding man with an overly weathered complexion snatched up a jug and a glass and provided her with a glass of water which she waved away and instead pointed to a wine glass which was quickly filled to the brim and passed to her. It was amazing to see a woman apparently in deep distress yet not spilling a single drop from the glass to her lips….

Chapter Fourteen

Mary- Belle turned her thoughts to the invited guests of this expedition. She had come here for a purpose and she was going to make sure that what she had come here to do was going to happen. She needed to focus her efforts.

She began making her way across to talk to Titus when she saw him get up and hurry away from his table and disappear up the staircase behind him. She guessed that he must be going to his room and although she wasn't sure where his room was, she knew that it must be somewhere on the first floor and this was too good an opportunity to pass up. She quickly made her way to the main door and then took the hallway stairs, she removed her shoes in order that she could move more quickly, and this dress although beautiful was proving impractical if you wanted to do anything in a hurry. She needed to arrive on the landing so that she could look along the minstrels' gallery before Titus made it to his room otherwise she would have no idea where he was and trying every room on the floor would waste precious time.

As she was a keen tennis player she was very fit, very fast and surprisingly strong and made it to the landing with ease. Looking across the gallery she cursed as the little figure of the vicar was nowhere to be seen. With her shoes still in her hand she started to make her way along the first leg of the gallery to her left. It was surprising just how loud the sounds of the assembled diners from below were up here. She looked up and took in the splendour of the beautiful painted ceiling, a famous feature of this house, from the gallery the fine work was so much clearer and the ornate gilding glowed golden, from the lights below giving off a surreal almost unfocussed warmth.

Then, out of the corner of her eye, she saw a sliver of light under a bedroom door. That had to be Titus. She started to make her way along the second leg of the gallery. Here there was a section of wall at the corner which formed a small pulpit arrangement from which she guessed the players performed. But there was a door here which was locked! She cursed again under her breath, there was nothing else for it she would need to retrace her steps around the gallery and approach the room from the same direction as Titus must have done. Time was ticking. She turned quickly and started back around in a half run but keeping her footfall light because she didn't want the people below to hear her; there were things she wanted to talk about with Titus that were best discussed in private. She knew there was every chance that a financial negotiation would need to take place but she was all right with that, these things often happened when people realised they had something that you wanted. But Mary-Belle was no one's fool and could drive a hard bargain with the best of them and she doubted very much that Titus Jennings would be considered the best of anything. She would get what she wanted she was sure of that.

Chapter Fifteen

Bailey was about to leave the room, he felt that he needed to have a sit down and really think about what he had discovered when it occurred to him that he hadn't yet told everyone about Titus and the note at all.

'Oh sorry everyone, I wouldn't want anyone to think that I was withholding any evidence. I have something here that I found on the body of Titus when I was checking him over. Bailey produced a discoloured piece of crumpled paper which was the note that Titus had discovered when he moved his napkin. Two thirds of the paper had a brownish tinge to it and some of the ink had run as well making it difficult to read. This caused Bailey to have to turn the paper around and peer intently at certain words but eventually he got the message out. Halfway through a middle aged woman in a light yellow dress raised her hand and asked where he had discovered the note because it looked as if it had fallen in the mud somewhere.

'Oh no dear lady!' exclaimed Bailey, 'no that's not mud, its blood' at which the poor woman collapsed in her chair and was immediately attended to by her fellow diners who looked over at the constable with incredulity. Bailey on the other hand appeared not to have noticed at all and merely made a remark about how difficult it was to read it now in this condition.

When he had finished Bailey addressed the room.

'Of course ladies and gentleman this means that someone was or is hopefully still here....when I say hopefully I mean from my point of view that it would be good because then I will be able to apprehend them as opposed to if they have already left, in which case I won't. Though I can see many people might be less comfortable with this idea, as it means that there is a murderer probably sat in this room right now'.

The realisation of this fact was not lost on the guests and people gave the person next to them, opposite them and behind them a quick nervous look just in case they were frothing at the mouth or their hands were covered in thick hair. But it appeared to everyone with some relief that at least the maniac wasn't sitting next to them.

'Now please, all of you enjoy the rest of your dinner. I need to retire to the study and collect my thoughts on what I have found out so far but I can tell you that I will remain calm and keep a blank mind on the whole situation.'

'Don't you mean an open mind PC Bailey?' drawled Mary-Belle Devine who had joined the room now quite recovered from her shocking discovery of the vicar.

'No I don't think so, blank is how I like to keep it.'

Mary-Belle slowly shook her head. There really was no fathoming the mind of Police Constable Bailey!

Chapter Sixteen

Crispin washed his hands quickly and then left the bathroom, choosing to return to the Great Hall through the side entrance favoured by the kitchen staff. As he approached the door he could hear that something was up. Suddenly as he reached to open the door it burst open towards him and a staff member barrelled into him almost knocking him over.

'I'm dreadfully sorry sir but someone appears to have been murdered in one of the bedrooms!' the servant blurted out the message as he passed him.

He entered the hall, he could hear a woman's voice from above his head screaming out something or other but her sobbing was making it difficult to understand the message. People were moving in all directions and he grabbed the nearest guest.

'What on earth has happened?'

'Oh it's terrible Mr Moorcock, Mary-Belle Devine has just informed us all that poor Titus has been murdered, what are we to do?!'

Crispin let go of the distraught woman and began to walk over to his table unsure whether he should follow the many who were trying to get up the stairs or should he remain here and wait to hear. While he pondered this for a moment he looked ahead and saw Lady Agatha striding across the room in the direction of the Policeman who it appeared had not noticed any of the chaos that was going on around him. He marvelled at this man's incompetence but thanked the stars at the same time; otherwise things could have turned out so very differently.

Chapter Seventeen

PC Bailey had set up his investigation room in the study where they had earlier taken the body of the unfortunate Major. This room worked well for him because it opened immediately off the Great Hall and the entrance to it was in clear sight of everyone so there was no chance at all that anyone could eavesdrop outside of the room without everyone else seeing them.

He had made an announcement that no one was allowed to leave Motley Hall that night and that included the staff. He requested that the doors and windows be secured and this had been done by Crawford and two trusted men handpicked by him. These same two men now guarded the two main exits from the house so all was as secure as Bailey could hope for given that he was the lone law enforcement Officer here.

He had confirmed this was now a murder investigation and he would have to conduct some immediate enquiries and said he hoped that everyone would cooperate fully with what he had to do.

The questioning was actually going very well. He had already been able to eliminate most of the staff early on and thirty-two of the guests because they all had strong alibis backed up and cross referenced with other people who had been on their tables at the times that both Monty had probably been poisoned and at the time when the murder of Titus must have taken place working backwards from the time that Mary-Belle called out from the minstrels' gallery.

He had also been lucky enough to find an elderly lady, Miss Partridge, who had been an office manager and was now being very helpful writing the investigation notes.

A number of the guests confirmed they had witnessed first-hand that Lady Agatha handed the glass to Monty and even heard her say 'make this your last drink'. Bailey thought about it for a while, surely she liked her nephew didn't she? Yes, he had seen her talking to him earlier and he had clearly been very fond of her. But there was this question of him being a spy. Did Lady Agatha know about that? He leant over and whispered 'Miss Partridge, can you make a note for me to remember to ask Lady Agatha did she know that her nephew was working for the secret service and was in fact a spy and if she did or even if she didn't was there any particular reason why she might have wanted to murder him'.

Miss Partridge looked up over her pince-nez, with her grey hair pinned so tightly to her head she looked like a judge to Bailey. Perfect he thought to himself, just perfect. 'Are you seriously going to ask her just like that PC Bailey?'

'Well yes I am trying to perfect a new type of interrogation technique. I call it direct questioning, what do you think?'

'If I am honest, I would say that it still has some way to go before it will be of any use to anyone if indeed it ever will.'

'Thank you Miss Partridge very kind comments I'm sure. Now from what I have been able to gather the only people who do not have good alibis for where they were at the times I am particularly interested in are Crispin Moorcock, Lady Agatha, Mary-Belle Devine and Edith Marleybone.'

'That's Marrowbone.'

'Oh yes Marrowbone. Anyway the point is this small group of people are the only ones who don't have proper alibis so I think we will start with Mr Moorcock.'

With that Bailey stood up and walked briskly to the study door and opened it. Beyond in the Great Hall the guests sat talking quietly in groups, the coffee course had been brought out. Bailey hoped that not only would he be able to get a pot of coffee for himself and his assistant but also that he would be able to get this sorted out before the cheese course. He had a real penchant for cheese. Some had moved away from their tables and had drawn up chairs to make bigger groups with others.

There appeared to be no reason for this but Bailey guessed that some people were just more sociable than others or perhaps they felt more comfortable in larger numbers. It appeared to him that people became really nervous when there was a murderer on the loose. He looked around the hall.

'Mr Moorcock, I wonder if you would be so good as to join me in the study.'

Crispin Moorcock was unsurprisingly surrounded by a small group of ladies. He smiled at them and walked smartly towards Bailey and the open study door beyond.

'Certainly Bailey, I hope you are actually getting somewhere with all of this as I was just saying to the ladies over there, this is really very upsetting for us all.'

Bailey gestured for him to come in, Crispin passed in front of the Constable and disappeared into the study, Bailey looked out to the people once more portraying what he hoped was a face of sincerity and then turned and entered the study closing the door silently behind him.

'Now then Mr Moorcock, if you would like to make yourself comfortable in that chair. I will sit here and just ask you a few questions about your whereabouts earlier this evening. My first question is did you speak to the Major before he died?'

'What?'

'No that's not quite what I meant Mr Meercroft.'

'Moorcock.'

'Exactly, Moorcock I meant, did you speak to Major Monty earlier on this evening, did you engage in any sort of conversation and if so what did you say to him?'

Crispin tapped his jacket pockets and located the packet of cigarettes he was looking for. He quickly took one and then offered them to Bailey and Miss Partridge; they both declined the offer with a shake of their heads.

'Oh you don't mind if I do though do you?

'No of course not Mr Moorcock, please go ahead, I'll get you an ashtray' Bailey moved across to the mantelpiece and retrieved a silver ashtray. It was art deco with a dancer stretching out behind her in a graceful arc while her dress spread out in front of her and made the bowl to collect the ash. Bailey thought how beautiful if was and how putting ash in it seemed almost criminal, but then if Crispin Moorcock turned out to be murderer that would be very fitting.

Moorcock took a puff on his cigarette and relaxed into the chair sitting slightly sideways with one arm draped over the back and with his legs crossed in front of him. He appeared to Bailey like an overgrown sixth former who had been brought to the headmaster's office and didn't really think they should have been.

'All right then Bailey what do you want to know. You can't think in your wildest dreams that I had anything to do with the death of that soldier do you? Yes, I did speak to the Major much earlier, before dinner in fact. We had a conversation about guns. He seemed keen to tell me about his military exploits and I humoured him. We talked for a short while and then he went off to refresh our drinks, while he was gone that delightful young woman Miss Devine came on the scene and so I engaged in a rather flirtatious conversation with her. She really is lovely and lives up to her name don't you think?'

'Er you mean Mary-Belle?'

'No Devine, dear God man I wonder how you follow any conversations at all sometimes!'

'Yes. Did you notice anyone else talking to the Major and in particular did you see Lady Agatha give him her drink and tell him to make this his last one?'

'Monty was quite a chap you know and he liked to talk to anyone who would listen, especially ladies, and there is nothing wrong with that of course. I definitely saw him talk to Miss Devine because she went over to him straight after talking to me. I got the impression that they had some history together because their conversation was close.'

'What do you mean by 'close' Mr Moorcock?'

'I mean they were closer together than people who have only met for the first time.'

'I see, I think. But you have already told me that Miss Devine is a very lovely individual which I agree to be true and also that the Major saw himself as quite the ladies' man so perhaps it was just that he wanted to get closer to her.'

'I will admit there is a possibility that could have been the way things happened. I only saw the Major's face and Miss Devine's back as she walked away from me towards him, so I wouldn't be able to say with any certainty what the expression might have been on Miss Devine's face but I could certainly see that the Major was smiling as she walked towards him.'

The Policeman considered the scenario for a moment. 'That doesn't really tell me much then does it Mr Moorcock as I can't imagine many men would be frowning if Miss Devine was walking towards them especially if she was dressed in the dress that she is wearing this evening.'

Miss Partridge gave a small but significant cough.

'Yes I suppose so Bailey, yes you have jolly good point there really. You know when I first met you I thought that you were not up to the job but when you come out with remarks like that I can see why you have got to where you are.'

The sarcasm in Moorcock's reply was completely lost on Bailey though Miss Partridge looked up from her note taking and met his gaze across the table with a look that would turn milk sour.

Bailey ploughed on with his questions. 'I have one more question concerning the Major and that is where were you exactly at the time that the poor man started to convulse and fall to the floor?'

'It's hard to remember exactly of course dear fellow. I remember that I had been standing quite near Lady Agatha. Mary-Belle was still talking to the Major but I was hoping to have another word with her myself when I heard the conversation that took place between Monty and his Aunt. She was suggesting to him that he had drunk rather too much and that he really should call it a night. However, she then held up her own glass and told him to make this his last one. I remember thinking at the time that giving him another drink was a very odd thing to do after just telling him that he had drunk enough but thought no more of it. Anyway the Major took the drink and Lady Agatha turned away from him and had returned to her table when the Major started making those awful noises as if he was suddenly in pain, which of course as it transpires he most certainly was.'

'And what did you do when you saw that he was in some sort of distress Mr Moorcock, what exactly did you do?'

'Nothing to be honest, there wasn't really any time. You know what it's like you see this sort of thing happen; when someone is having a problem you want to help, well of course you do, but things happen so fast you become just an observer and that's what happened here. Before I knew it the poor man was on the floor and Mary-Belle was screaming and then fainting'. He paused for a moment and then looked straight at PC Bailey. A look passed over the face of Crispin Moorcock, a look that didn't come very often. It was the look of revelation.

'PC Bailey, I don't want to be the one casting any sort of accusations here you understand but don't you think it is more than a coincidence that it was Mary-Belle Devine who was standing next to the Major just before he died and then screamed the place down before collapsing and not too much later in the same evening the woman can be heard screaming murder at the top of her voice as she was the one that discovered the body of Titus. Now don't you think that is all a little coincidental?'

'To be honest with you Meercroft, this will probably come as a bit of a shock to you but that had not occurred to me.'

Moorcock managed to raise one eyebrow but out of the corner of his vision he also caught the expression on Miss Partridge's face and thought better of his initial response.

'It's Moorcock and you can't be expected to think of everything you know, this is complex. I am sure that it would have occurred to you before long. On this occasion I have merely speeded up the logical thought process.'

He looked again at Partridge and saw that she approved of this response but it was clear that he was on a last warning for making any sort of fun at the Constable's expense.

'That's all I want to ask you regarding the Major at this point Sir'

Moorcock went to rise from his seat but while he was still taking the weight on his arms, Bailey shot out his hand and held it up in front of him as if he was controlling traffic.

'However, I still want to ask you some questions about the Vicar Mr Titus Jennings, you seem to have forgotten that we have been unlucky this evening and not only had the death of the Major which has turned out to be a poisoning but also Titus Jennings who was most definitely murdered.'

'Ah yes of course. Silly me what was I thinking? Naturally you will want to ask me questions about that murder as well.

'And when I say the second murder of the vicar, I don't actually mean that the vicar was murdered for a second time. Oh no. What I mean is that he was the second victim of murder.'

'Yes, yes I had rather got that PC Bailey.'

Bailey looked relieved that he had cleared up that point and then continued

'So Mr Moorcock, did you notice anything suspicious about Reverend Jennings either before the Major died or after for that matter? Did you see him talking to anyone in an odd way? Did you see anyone talking to him perhaps in a murderous way which at the time you may have passed it off as being nothing of importance but now that his body has been discovered in his room covered in blood you now think that there may be some significance to an earlier conversation? Oh, and while you are thinking about all of that, did you murder Reverend Jennings?'

Miss Partridge looked up from her notes once more but this time instead of the frown that she had been giving earlier to Moorcock, she now looked at the Policeman with a look of utter amazement and shook her head slowly.

Bailey saw the look on her face and also on the face of Crispin Moorcock. 'Ah yes I forgot to say Moorcock, I am trying out a new questioning approach which I am hoping, when I have ironed out the teething troubles, that it might be adopted by Police forces across the country. I call it direct questioning.'

'Bailey', started Moorcock 'May I begin by asking you why I would kill the Vicar? You have only to ask yourself the question why on earth would I do it? He was a lowly Vicar from a lowly parish or in fact without a parish at all at the moment. He had latched himself on to help Lady Agatha with her trips abroad and had no money of his own to speak off. What could I possibly gain from his death?'

'It is a good point Mr Moorcock. The direct questioning technique probably still needs some work to finely tune it but I am sure that if I were to ask the real murderer such a direct question then I am sure that they would crack under the surprise. But as you say, on the face of it there doesn't appear to be any good reason for you to kill him. There is still the question of the photographs that were found thrown all over the floor of his bedroom.'

'What photographs?'

Bailey stuttered for a moment but decided that the brief details of what was contained in the photographs probably couldn't cause too much of problem for the RAF if he were to reveal it to his suspects here, hundreds of miles away from the air bases.

'They were pictures of military air bases in the desert. They have been identified by Lady Agatha who said she arranged for Titus to take the pictures from an aircraft on her behalf.'

Crispin Moorcock shifted his position in his seat. He now sat upright in the chair and was leaning forward taking in every detail of what was being discussed. His body language had changed completely from the almost nonchalant to the very attentive. Bailey had noticed the difference but had no idea why the death of the Vicar seemed to generate more interest than the death of the Major who had turned out to be a spy.

'I can't think why the photographs are significant and they mean nothing to me Bailey. Have you considered at all that the photographs may have been thrown over the body after the deed had been carried out?'

'Yes I have considered that but I can't think of a reason why anyone would do that, can you?'

'Maybe it's some kind of message; killers often do that don't they? Like a calling card, a reason why they have carried out the dastardly act.'

'If you say so Moorcroft. Anyway for now I can't think of a reason why you would want to have killed Titus for as far as I can make out you didn't know him before this evening and even though a number of people heard you getting slightly irritated over the fact that he was questioning you about late payment for this trip, I do not believe you would have murdered him over that. So you are free to go and join the rest of the party and I must get myself and Miss Partridge some refreshments before we continue with our questions.'

Crispin arose from his chair and walked back towards the study door. Bailey followed him and let him back out into the Great Hall. Once again a sea of faces greeted the Policeman.

'Ladies and Gentlemen I can assure you that the questions are going very well. I am just going to arrange some coffee for myself and my assistant Miss Partridge and then we will continue with Miss Edith Marrowbone.'

At that point Burrows who had overheard Bailey snapped his fingers and sent a servant off to the kitchen to prepare a pot of coffee and petit fours to be sent to the study with two cups. He nodded to Bailey that all had been taken care of and received an acknowledgment back from the Constable in the form of a quick smile. Bailey for his part was already preparing to receive Edith Marrowbone who was moving towards the study for her turn in the hot seat.

'Ah Miss Marrowbone. It is Miss isn't it?'

'Yes PC Bailey you are correct. I have not been without my suitors you understand but there has been no man yet that I have been willing to fully commit to. Actually, there is one but there is nothing more to be said about that. Now tell me, you said out there in front of everyone that the questioning has gone well. By that am I to assume that you have a firm lead to go on? Are you in fact close to discovering who the murderer is?'

There was a faint knock at the study door and a servant arrived with the tray of coffee. On seeing that there were only two cups on the tray Bailey asked the servant to bring four extra cups in case the current or a future suspect might want to enjoy some refreshment during their questioning. The servant retired for the extra cups. In the meantime, Miss Partridge poured coffee for Bailey and Miss Marrowbone. She didn't actually like coffee but Bailey had failed to ask her about her preference which had annoyed her a little. She would order tea from the servant when he returned.

'Now Miss Marrowbone, I did mention that the questioning had gone well but that was just to say exactly that. I have not finished talking to the small group of people who do not have their alibis confirmed by other members of the party. I would like to say that I have discovered who the perpetrator of these crimes is but at the present time I have not been able do this. By the way did you kill either Major Monty Fortescue-Smythe or Titus Jennings or are you in fact guilty of murdering both of them?'

There was an audible groan from Miss Partridge and Edith almost choked being mid-swallow when Bailey asked the question.

On placing her cup back on the saucer Edith looked over to the expectant expression of the Constable.

'Dear me PC Bailey, is this your line of questioning? I was under the impression that you were undertaking a series of questions to build up a picture of the whereabouts of people at the times when these murders must have taken place. I didn't dream for a moment that you would take such a direct line of questioning. So in answer to your question, no I didn't kill either of them. I'm sorry to disappoint and all that.'

'Ah you see Miss Marrowbone how education comes in so useful. With a lot of other people that I have used my new direct questioning technique on, they have always looked shocked. But you have immediately identified that I am using this technique. Well done and thank you for your answer.'

'I am glad to oblige though frankly I am not sure I entirely follow your thought process. I merely commented about the fact that you had used a direct question because you had, in fact, used a direct question. I was not aware that it was a technique.'

'In any case dear lady, it clears that matter up. However, before you go I would like to ask you where you were at the time Mary-Belle Devine called out following the discovery of Titus Jennings. You see I checked with the other diners on your table and they were all very clear that you were not in the room at the time that she called but that you returned very shortly afterwards.'

'I was in the bathroom PC Bailey. I spilled a small amount of the soup on my sleeve and wanted to wash it out as soon as possible to avoid a stain. See, here, there is still a dull red spot. It's very annoying really, who knows when we will be able to find somewhere to wash our clothes properly on this trip? My hope is that the ship will have a decent laundry facility. I returned directly from the bathroom and passed no one in the corridor and then I heard the commotion being caused by that American woman. At first I couldn't make out exactly what was going on as people in the room were already beginning to move upstairs to help and so I waited at the table. Do you think that I should have gone upstairs as well?'

'No Miss Marrowbone, you did the right thing to wait. To be honest there were far too many people upstairs who were making it very difficult for me to do my job properly. Thank you for clearing up where you were. It is a shame no one else saw you but I am happy at the present time to accept your word. Once again I can see no real reason why you would have wanted to murder the Vicar. I forgot to ask you if you had a conversation with the Major at all?'

'I had a brief conversation with him. As a matter of fact, he flirted with me a little. I also heard him later talking in the company of some other guests; he was a very good talker and held his audience well with very amusing stories of his bravery in the field.'

'Thank you Miss Marrowbone, you are free to go.'

PC Bailey once again opened the door from the study but once Miss Marrowbone had left he closed it again without asking for the next suspect to enter. Instead he turned to Miss Partridge who had her head down finishing off her notes of the interview.

'Tell me what you think Miss Partridge.'

'About what in particular PC Bailey? If you are referring to Miss Marrowbone I would have to say that she is very nice but she is also very intelligent and could easily be putting on an act for you.'

Bailey nodded and Miss Partridge continued.

'It is all a little too convenient that she was unseen going or retuning to the bathroom if indeed she was there at all but I also fail to see why she would have wanted to harm the vicar when there appears to be no obvious connection between them. She also made very little contact with the Major so she appears to be in the clear unless you can turn up something else. Of course I am not the professional here Constable and am only giving my opinion as you have asked for it.'

Bailey was about to reply that he was very happy for her to voice her opinion and also that he agreed with what she said, however none of this happened because at that moment the door to the study opened and Lady Agatha Plantagenet swept into the room and closed the door behind her.

'The evening is beginning to drag Bailey and I have a lot to do before we can all leave in the morning. I would therefore like to get my questioning out of the way as quickly as possible. I have no interest in the cheese course and to be honest I think it would be a very good idea if everyone took my lead and retired soon so that we all get a fairly decent night's sleep. Of course given the events that have taken place here this evening and the fact that you don't appear to be any closer discovering who the culprit is, there is always the chance that we will be murdered in our beds!'

Lady Agatha halted abruptly and bowed her head for a moment before returning her gaze to Bailey once more.

'To be honest for a moment Bailey, I am finding it increasingly difficult to keep up this façade in front of everyone. My dearest nephew has, it would appear, been murdered and yet I must keep up a strong appearance because it is vital that this trip happens and so we must be off in the morning otherwise we will miss our embarkation time and the

Gloriana will sail without us. 'Time and Tide', as they say 'waits for no man'. So I implore you Bailey to finish your questions with me as soon as possible, so that I may bring this ghastly evening to a close and perhaps salvage some of my reputation for running a tight ship which, at the present time, is in tatters. I am also not quite as young as I was and I really need to get some sleep.'

'Lady Agatha, I wasn't quite ready to begin my questioning with you but since you have arrived I would suggest that you now sit down here and I will get on with it.

As to your comment about being leaving in the morning, it won't be possible and that's not because we will all be 'murdered in our beds' tonight as you put it, but rather that I won't be able to let anyone leave until I have discovered the culprit. So let's hope I do it soon.

To be honest I am in two minds over you, your Ladyship. On the one hand the Major was your nephew, so do I really believe that you would invite him to join you with all of these members of the public and then give him a glass in full view of everyone and tell him this would be his last drink, which was poisoned? Do I also think that you would murder your assistant just before you left for a safari in front of all of these people when surely you would have had more opportunity on the trip? There must have been many times before this evening that you would have had the chance to kill him if you so wished. But on the other hand perhaps you are very clever and doing that bluff thing where it's too obvious when all the time it isn't really at all. Yes, I don't mind telling you it's a real dilemma.'

Lady Agatha had seated herself in the chair as had the suspects before her. She sat very calmly with her hands folded in her lap waiting for Bailey to finish and now that her time had arrived she unfolded her hands and rose from the chair to stand fully in front of the Constable who, on seeing her expression, knew that he was in for it.

'PC Bailey. I asked my dear friend Inspector Lansdowne, if he could see fit to send along a Police Officer, because, with so much going on in the world these days, I felt that it might be in order to have someone official to oversee the crowd as it were, not to mention the death threats. When I asked the dear man that small favour I could never have imagined that we would end up at this juncture where my nephew and my assistant both lay cold and silent somewhere in the environs of the kitchen in this house and you are our only hope of catching the criminal. If all of that was not enough to cause me to slip into a deepest depression, I am now confronted by you informing me that I may actually be a suspect in the murders. I would suggest my dear man that you quickly sort out your 'two minds' because it seems to me that you are having enough trouble with one!'

Bailey leaned over to Miss Partridge 'I don't think I am going to go with the direct questioning technique at this stage of things.'

'I think that is possibly the wisest decision you have made this evening Constable.'

'Lady Agatha…'

'No PC Bailey, I will not listen to any more of this rambling. If you think that I poisoned my nephew in plain sight of everyone and if you think I then followed Titus to his room and murdered him then arrest me man! But before you do, let me ask you this question; why would I murder Titus for photographs if that is indeed what this is all about when they were mine in the first place? Judging from the look of surprise that I now see on your face, you had forgotten that small detail constable.'

'It's true Lady Agatha that with all the things that have occurred I had quite forgotten and I have to agree that if the photographs were the reason for Titus to be murdered then that now makes no sense. However, there is something that I would like to discuss with you before you go.'

Bailey moved across to some papers that were lying on the arm of the settee. He took them up and after sorting through them for a moment, he walked back and placed a single sheet of paper in front of her on the table.

'These are papers that I brought with me from Exeter this morning. I didn't really bother to look through them but the sergeant said that they might come in handy at some point and I am thinking this might be one of those points.'

Lady Agatha looked down at the sheet. The print was fairly small and so she took up her handbag and produced her spectacles. She returned to the sheet which read as follows;

The Times
14th August 1935

Sources in the Far East and Africa have reported that certain valuable artefacts have been removed from the tombs of the Pharaohs in Egypt and have ended up in the hands of private collectors around the world.

At the present time it has been impossible to ascertain who is masterminding the operation but a number of local people have been arrested carrying out the thefts.

It is hoped that with questioning these persons will provide vital information that will enable the authorities to bring this very lucrative trade to an early end.

Bailey watched Agatha for a moment and let her take in the contents of the newspaper cutting 'I wonder what you make of that your Ladyship?'

'My question to you Bailey is why it was given to you in the first place. But yes I am happy to make a comment. The fact is that not everyone who is working in the areas of the digs is either licensed or honest and in most cases they are neither. This has led to a number of very valuable and irreplaceable items having been taken, stolen, and there has been no trace of them since. In some cases, the items have been fairly large and yet no one appears to have seen anything. Our digs are of course with the full permission of the Egyptian Minister of the Interior and all fully above board.'

'I see, and if I requested a look at this permission would you be able to produce it?'

'Yes of course PC Bailey. It will be with the paperwork for the trip which..'

She stopped in mid-sentence and brought her hand to her mouth as she reminded herself that her assistant was no more.

'Oh dear, excuse me PC Bailey but the image of Titus laying up there in all that blood has just come back to me. I need to sit down for a moment.'

'Of course Lady Agatha. I have no further questions. Why not take a few minutes to compose yourself and then perhaps you would like to join the rest of the guests for a short while. I have only one more person to talk to and then perhaps I will be able to shed a little more light on what is going on.'

Miss Partridge leant forward and offered a handkerchief to Agatha who took one look at it and produced an altogether far more luxurious lace affair complete with the initials 'AP' embroidered on one corner in blue cotton. She dabbed at her eyes briefly and then puckering up the item in her hand she placed it over her nose and blew long and loud with a noise that more closely resembled the mating call of a Bull Elephant rather than the delicate blowing of a lady.

'That's better. I feel much better Bailey. Please do not stand on ceremony with your questions, you must bring this to a conclusion and you must do it soon.'

With that Agatha left the room. Bailey wasted no time and called out for Mary Belle-Devine to join them. A few moments passed and then Bailey called for a second time but there was still no sign.

'Has anyone seen Miss Devine?' Bailey was starting to look anxious.

'I'm here Mr Policeman. I simply wanted to take some air. I have been talking to the guard on the door, he was good enough to open the door and let me get some fresh air. Is that all right with you?'

'Yes of course Miss Devine though my instructions to the servants manning the entrances were that they should not open the doors on any account. I will make a note to remind them of the importance of that fact though I am sure in your case he thought it was highly unlikely that you were going to make a run for it in that dress.'

Back in the study PC Bailey remained standing while Mary-Belle made herself comfortable. He offered her some refreshment but she had declined as did Miss Partridge.

Bailey opened the conversation.

'Miss Devine, I have to say that on the face of things there is strong evidence that you may well be involved in the deaths of these two men here this evening. You were seen by a number of people talking to the Major in a very friendly way and then later you were standing next to him when he took the drink from his aunt and promptly died. You were also the person who found the body of the vicar. Why were you up there in any case, were you looking for him?'

I have made no secret at all PC Bailey that I have been friends with Monty for over three years. I first met him when I was with my husband and we have met since. I was very pleased to see him here this evening and enjoyed his company for over half an hour before he took that glass from Lady Agatha and then and then...'

'Oh dear, please Miss Devine not you as well. It appears that everyone is getting upset recounting the events that have taken place and while I appreciate that they are still fresh in their minds and also the fact that this man was a friend of yours I could really do with people remaining calm under questioning so that we can get to the bottom of exactly what went on here this evening.'

Mary-Belle Devine sat silently with her head bowed for a few minutes and then tilting her head upwards so that Bailey could look straight into her beautiful face now streaked with the evidence of her emotions, she sniffed back her tears and composed herself.

'You're right PC Bailey. I must remain calm for Monty's sake, I must. Now you wish to know why I was upstairs. Well that's fairly easy, I wanted to have private word with Titus because I wanted to negotiate with him the best cabin that I possibly could. I had already spoken to some of the other passengers and it was clear to me that most, if not all, of the good cabins had already been allocated. I had only had a brief opportunity to talk to him earlier at pre-dinner drinks and we were still discussing hat boxes when he was called away by Lady Agatha. So I therefore reasoned that I would have to be very persuasive if I was going to succeed and I do my most persuasive work when I am alone and uninterrupted if you understand my meaning. In the case of Jennings of course I didn't expect that I would need to be offering my charms to win him around but I do also have a great deal of money and I am sure that even a lowly parish vicar can do with a little extra cash.

So that was my plan. I saw him leave the dining room and make his way to the stairs. I decided that to follow him up the same staircase would put me in the view of most of the room so I opted for the smaller staircase which leads from the hallway. I walked around the gallery but the door was locked and so I had to retrace my steps which delayed me and by the time I arrived at Mr Jennings' bedroom he was already dead. I had called out to him because I heard noises as I came along the landing but I didn't see anyone at all so how did they leave his room undetected?'

'Oh that mystery is easily solved Miss, there was a second door over the far side of his bedroom. He had allocated the better rooms to the paying guests leaving him the servant's room which connected to the servants landing and stairs via one door while the other opened out to the gallery. If you really disturbed his assailant, that is how they managed to leave the room without you seeing them. Of course the other option is that you were the first and only person who visited the vicar in which case it was you who murdered him.'

Mary-Belle remained calm and looked from Miss Partridge and then back to Bailey while she absorbed what the Policeman was saying.

'Yes PC Bailey it is indeed one of the options. Do you think that there is more than one murderer here tonight?'

'If that is the case then this is going to take all night and I was hoping to join the others for the cheese course!' Bailey realised that this had probably not come out as he had wanted it to but he pressed on regardless.

'What I mean is that I am working on the theory that both men were murdered by the same person though what the connection is between the two of them at the moment is a mystery to me. But if I am right and it is the same person then I should be able to clear this up before too much longer.'

Miss Partridge's eyes peeked out over the top of her spectacles but she said nothing.

'And you think that I may be that one person PC Bailey?'

'Before I left Exeter I was handed a number of letters and papers by my desk sergeant. He said it was sent from Inspector Lansdowne who is a good friend of Lady Agatha'. Anyway, in amongst the papers I found this, which I would like you to have a look at.'

Bailey once again fetched the pile of papers and selected the one he knew concerned this lady.

Pan-Pacific Telegraphic Company

To: Inspector Lansdowne, Scotland Yard, **England**
Date: December 2nd 1936
Subject: Devine Marybelle (Mrs)

He glanced at the face of Mary-Belle and read on.

Further to your request for additional information: **STOP**: Be advised that no new evidence has been uncovered surrounding the suspected drowning of Dwight Devine last June: **STOP**: Only skeleton crew and wife of deceased on board at time of incident: **STOP**: Further questioning may shed new light: **STOP**:Confirmation that Wife of deceased inherits entire estate of $173 Million uncontested: **STOP**: Hope of some use. Gut feelings tell me she did it as discussed; **STOP**:+++++++++++++
Lieutenant Harsher - County Police Marshall
Pompano, Florida USA

'I wonder if you would like to make any comment Miss Devine?'

But Mary-Belle wasn't listening to PC Bailey, her thoughts were a long way from Motley Hall. She remembered how hot the sun was on that beautiful day in late June, the 'Mary – Belle' a fifty-five-foot statement of pure luxury.

'It is true that my dear husband Dwight was lost at sea when we were on our yacht. It is a matter of public record and I was interviewed at some length by the local police at the time including this Lieutenant Harsher person. I got the impression at the time that he didn't like me very much and thought that I was lying. His comment on this telegram confirms that don't you think? But why are you showing me this now PC Bailey. Why does this have anything to do with what happened here tonight?'

Bailey looked lost in thought.

'Miss Devine, can I ask you what the name of the yacht was?'

'It was and still is called the 'Mary-Belle''

'Crikey, well who would have thought it, what is the chance of that? I wonder how many women Mr Devine started up a relationship with before he found one with the same name as his yacht!'

'No PC Bailey the yacht was named after…oh it really doesn't matter I guess. Anyway you haven't answered my question, why show me this?'

'My point in showing you this Miss Devine is that if I am to believe what the Lieutenant believes happened, then you may have already been involved in the murder of someone and therefore as they say once a murderer, always a murderer.'

'I'm sure I have never heard that particular phrase PC Bailey but all right I see where you are coming from. I would like to point out though that if I did kill my husband and I am by no means saying that I did, then it would be safe to imagine that I did it for the money wouldn't you say?'

'Yes Miss Devine I would say that was the most obvious reason for doing it'.

'And if that was the reason PC Bailey then why have I carried out these two murders tonight as in neither case can I see that I would have benefitted financially can you?'

Bailey looked crestfallen but then quickly brightened and with a smile spreading across his face he stood up and moved towards the door.

'Miss Devine you are correct. I can't see any connection and to be honest I am delighted to say that as I never thought it could possibly have been such a charming and attractive woman as you are.'

'Why thank you PC Bailey. I feel that I am blushing'.

Mary-Belle left the room and closing the door he turned to speak to Miss Partridge who was already standing busily brushing the crumbs off her dress from the petit fours that had accompanied the coffee.

'Constable Bailey I will write up these notes so that they may be of some use to you though, to be honest, I must say you have the most unorthodox style of interrogation and questioning that I have ever seen or heard of. How you have picked up anything of use from speaking to those suspects I do not know.'

'Thank you Miss Partridge you have been of great service to the constabulary this evening and I will make sure that it doesn't go unnoticed when I have a chance to talk to my superiors. In the meantime, please join the rest of the party as I noticed the servants were just coming out with the cheese boards so our timing for finishing the questions could not have been better.'

They both left the study and as Bailey was about to address the party he saw Edith Marrowbone enter the Great Hall from the far side. She fixed him with a stare and then returned to her seat at the table. Bailey surveyed the room while he informed everyone that although he felt he now had a better understanding of the movements of the main suspects he had as yet been unable to discover who the villain was but felt sure it was only a matter of time.

He noticed that all of the remaining suspects were not in the room, and then one by one they returned. First Lady Agatha entered through the main doors while a moment later Mary Belle slunk in through the side door that led to the bathroom corridor. Bailey continued to watch for a full minute and then another, people started to stop their conversations and once again turn in his direction but still he stood looking about him. After four minutes had passed everyone was silent watching the Policeman and then he spoke quickly and clearly so that everyone along the back of the room could hear the urgency in his question.

'Where is Crispin Moorcock? Gentleman I must ask for your assistance, we must find him and quickly. I believe that his life is in danger!'

Men started to leave their respective tables and spurred on by more shouts of 'quickly look everywhere' and 'he must be found' from the constable they headed off in all directions to track down Crispin Moorcock. Within a couple of minutes', shouts could be heard coming from all over the house as the searchers spread out. Shadows could be seen moving around on the minstrel's gallery as each bedroom door was opened and the rooms quickly checked. The entire first floor was searched thoroughly in less than ten minutes but still no sign of the banker's son could be found.

Then as some on the men returned to the Great Hall shrugging their shoulders as if the man had vanished, a cry went up and the side door opened revealing a middle aged man with a flushed face.

'He's here; Moorcock is along here in a cupboard. I think he has been shot!'

Chapter Eighteen

The questioning had gone even better than he thought. He knew that Bailey was a mile off having any clue what was going on and the ridiculous idea of 'direct questioning' that the idiot was trying out was a whole new level of incompetence. Moorcock had seen the look on Miss Partridge's face, the woman who Bailey had introduced as the note taker, and it was a look that told him even she couldn't believe her own ears.

So now it was time to close things here. Even though Bailey was more than useless, people were now on edge and when people are like that they become more observant and that was only going to make his job harder and that annoyed him.

This cover of the upper class twit was working like a charm. He was actually starting to like this chap. He had used many characters over the many missions he had undertaken and this one was far and away the most fun. He liked the way he could poke fun at the English upper class and everyone thought that it was all right.

'Well I just need to pop along to the you know where 'the king of Spain can't take his horses' if you understand my meaning and then we'll all get some more jolly drinks before the cheese board and the coffee come around what?'

Still laughing at his ridiculous saying for using the bathroom, he moved away from the table and made his way into the corridor. It was impressive how sturdy these old doors were and how almost the entire hubbub of the Great Hall was lost the moment that the door was closed.

He decided to move to the far end of the corridor past double doors that led to the respective male and female bathrooms. It was then that he first noticed the brass handle set in the wall. It was flush with the panelling and very easy to miss. He lifted the handle and turned it slowly. It wasn't locked, a good start. A door clicked open revealing a dark space inside the wall. He took a quick look inside and could see that it was some sort of cupboard, an aroma of stale soapy water and polish told him that the cleaning staff must be using this room as their storeroom which made sense of course being this close to the bathrooms. He could make out objects in the gloom and snapping on the light switch confirmed his suspicion as he looked at the mop and bucket and a number of dusters, tins of polish and spare light bulbs on the shelf which ran along the back wall. To one side there was a pile of cushions which he assumed had been put in there to store. He switched off the light and removed the bulb placing it next to the tins he had seen a moment before.

He stepped inside and was fully enclosed inside the cupboard when he sensed that someone had entered the corridor. He turned slowly and looked out keeping the door slightly ajar.

'And so we meet in our official capacity' he said in his own soft voice. A style he had cultivated himself over his time in training. He found that a soft voice disarmed people and gave you an edge. In his line of work that was important and often gave you the split second you needed to emerge as the survivor.

He opened the door a little further and signalled the other person to come out of sight of the corridor. They followed and both stood facing each other in the semi-darkness.

'You must realise that I do not have the package. Bailey has them now. He doesn't realise what he is holding on to so it might not be too difficult to retrieve them.'

'I understand. But what is your intention once you have them?'

'To complete my mission, what possible other outcome could there be. Do you think that I would sell them or something?'

There was no answer.

'I see.'

The door opened again and male voices could be heard, two of them. They had obviously been drinking because they spoke both very loudly and with a slur a sure sign that the wine from Algy's cellar had not been wasted. Moorcock closed the cupboard door almost completely leaving the two of them standing in the dark. The men had taken the door into the male bathroom; their now muffled conversation could still be heard.

Minutes passed and then the men re-emerged back into the corridor and made their way back into the hall restoring the silence of the corridor once more. Moorcock reached for the door once again and let enough light back in from the corridor so that he could just make out the facial features of his fellow agent.

'We lost contact with you. Herr Greunig was worried that something had happened to you and that is why they sent me. They even thought you might have turned. Look here.'

Moorcock took a note from his coat. He shook it out and in the dim light now coming in through the door. He read out the message from Greunig. When he had finished he looked up and smiled.

'You must understand, the Fuhrer himself is interested in this package but then you already know that. We must now work together to make the retrieval and to leave. Is that understood and agreed?'

'Of course, with two of us this will be a simple operation. I have already arranged transport for later this evening. We have probably two hours to make our plans and carry them out. Do you have a cigarette?'

Moorcock felt inside his jacket pocket and produced a pack. He shook out two, replaced the pack and took out his lighter. The sudden light from the flame illuminated them both for a second or two and then he snapped down the lid and passed it to his now accomplice. They fumbled the transfer and the cigarette disappeared to the floor.

'Damn it, wait a moment' said the other voice as they bent down to retrieve it.

'What next?' said Moorcock as the agent stood up again, the end of the cigarette glowing in their hand.

'This.'

Moorcock was suddenly aware that their bodies had become very close but no, that wasn't a body, it was softer. His last thought was 'this is a cushion, why a cushion?' and then just as the bullet exploded into his heart, he worked it out.

Chapter Nineteen

Howls went up around the room as the realisation that the murderer was still at large gripped everyone. The room suddenly appeared, to many, to be colder and the shadows longer in the corners than before. People began to imagine crouching figures in every gloomy nook and cranny.

Once again Lady Agatha led the charge but this time quickly followed by Bailey. They followed the flushed man back along the corridor to what appeared to be some sort of cupboard just beyond the bathrooms.

Bailey looked around for the switch and flicked it but it appeared that it wasn't working. He looked around for a member of staff and asked them to find a replacement. They wouldn't go in themselves but informed Bailey that the bulbs were on the shelf inside this very cupboard. Bailey reached in and found the one that had been removed. He screwed the bulb back into place and snapped on the light.

There, in the back of this small dingy room lay the body of Crispin Moorcock. A pillow had been placed over his chest but it was clear that he was dead. His lifeless face turned towards the wall, his arms and legs all twisted out of position as if he had been folded into this small space. That was the thing that struck Bailey the most as he looked at the body. Yes, he had been folded, not carried.

The front of his shirt was almost completely soaked in his blood and it was very clear that he had been shot. The remains of the cushion lay nearby. Bailey picked it up and examined it for a moment. It had been used as a muffler to mask the noise of the shot and the solid construction of the house would have been sufficient to deaden the noise from the people sitting in the Great Hall. Whoever had done this, thought Bailey, they had known what they were doing.

Bailey looked around the body and noticed that under the left hand was a piece of paper. He picked it up and examined it. It was a letter that read as follows;

It is now imperative that we are in receipt of the photographs with all speed. You are likely to find that your agent in the field is far from accommodating as they have developed their own agenda.

They are unaware that you are anything but a backup in this mission. I instruct you to make the acquisition of the information your utmost priority.

If everything is not in order, then you are to dispatch the agent once this transaction has been completed.

Do not fail, the party rewards those that are of service.

I await your safe return to my office with anticipation.

Frank Greunig

Bailey looked at the note and considered it. So not only did he have a murderer on the loose but it looked as if there were at least two agents here tonight. Crowd control was never supposed to be this hard was it?

He folded the paper in half and then turned and stepped out of the cupboard. He was about to close the door when he saw the kitchen porters arriving with a trolley.

He nodded to them and left them to it as he made his way, once again, back into the main room. He would have to face the people but he was rapidly running out of ideas. He had one though. He would sit down with some cheese and have a good think like his sergeant told him to do. In fact, he said think three times so he would do just that. It would give him more time to collect his ideas, and more time to eat more cheese.

Then he would gather everyone together and let them know his thoughts.

Chapter Twenty – Denouement

'It has been a very harrowing night and I know that for some of you it will take a great deal of time to get over what you have experienced and for that I wholeheartedly apologise. However, I feel that now I have enough facts to be able to piece together what has happened here and to bring this to a close.'

There was a general rumble around the guests which suggested that they were, at the very least; surprised by this bold statement from the Police Officer given that up until now he appeared to be completely clueless.

'Ladies and Gentlemen let us think about the reasons why people commit murder. Money is always a strong factor, jealousy, hate, revenge, love even. They are all good reasons and we must look at what has happened here to see if we can find evidence of any of those reasons and see if they will lead us to why someone has committed these heinous acts this evening.

But let us go back for a moment, over the series of events that happened. Firstly, during the drinks we had before our dinner, often referred to as the 'pre-dinner drinks', most of you saw Major Montague Fortescue-Smythe take a drink from his aunt Lady Agatha which, was not his usual drink by the way, and heard her tell him to 'make this his last drink'. I have always believed it is a mistake to mix your drinks and here is a good example. As we now all know it was indeed his last drink for it had been liberally laced with prussic acid with the result that the poor Major died shortly after drinking it in pain on the floor.

When I searched the body I discovered that the Major had another side to his character that we didn't know about, he was in fact working for the British secret service and I believe he was on a mission here to thwart a German spy from infiltrating the ranks of this safari party because that's what it said on that piece of paper that I found on him.

Now you may wonder why a trained spy would be so foolish to drink prussic acid but you see Lady Agatha's favourite drink was Amaretto, which is strongly flavoured with almonds which would have masked the signature smell of this deadly poison.

Then even before we had finished the main course we all heard the cries of Miss Mary-Belle Devine who had apparently discovered the body of Titus Jennings who had been expertly slain in his room and a number of pictures were found strewn around the bedroom and over his body.

I couldn't think of a reason why the pictures would have been thrown over the room after killing the vicar when Lady Agatha made it clear that they were of military installations and would be valuable in the right hands. Then when we moved the body on to the bed I noticed another couple of pictures were actually under the body.

This made me think again and I finally arrived at the conclusion that the pictures were on the floor before Titus was killed. This convinced me that the pictures had been dropped somehow in the struggle and they were what the murderer was after. If we are to believe Miss Devine's story, then perhaps she disturbed the killer before they could collect them up after killing Titus.

And then following my questioning of the suspects I noticed that Crispin Moorcock was no longer in the room and after a search his body was discovered in that cupboard which the cleaners use. He had been shot at very close range with the killer using a cushion to er well cushion the noise of the gun.

Now how do my suspects fit into the story?'

Bailey turned to face the line of suspects that he had assembled in front of the entrance doors. Lady Agatha had refused to stand and had drawn up a chair as she could see that this was going to take a while. She sat half turned towards the room and reminded him of picture he had seen of Queen Victoria in a book somewhere. She had that same expression on her face that whatever he said in the next few minutes, she was not going to be amused.

'Lady Agatha Plantagenet, why would you want to kill your own nephew? Could it have been that you are the German infiltrator and that you discovered somehow that Monty was a spy; you knew you had no other option but to get him out of the way if you were going to make contact and obtain those photographs of the military installations?' Bailey paused and looked confused for a moment, a face that many had seen countless times. He continued 'At first I thought aha! So that was why you invited Monty to join you on this trip so that you could murder him. But then I thought but surely if you knew he was spy before he came here this evening then having him here at all would only complicate your mission. I also had a second thought'

'Wonders will never cease PC Bailey, two thoughts on the same subject running consecutively' snorted Lady Agatha.

'Thank you your Ladyship. Anyway my second thought was this.... Titus Jennings was your assistant and in fact it was you that had arranged for him to go up in the aeroplane in the first place so if he was your contact then you already knew him and that he had the photographs so you wouldn't have needed to have a note from anyone to tell you about your contact because he already was your contact wasn't he or have I missed something?'

'Perhaps single thoughts would be better Bailey as you have certainly lost me at this point but I think what you are trying to say is that there would not have been any need for a clandestine meeting with a code word because I already knew Titus and that he had the photographs if indeed I was the contact and wanted them. Is that about it dear boy?'

'Precisely Lady Agatha. And it is for this reason that I do not believe that you are the murderer'

'Well I am relieved that you have...'

'However Lady Agatha' Bailey interrupted 'I do believe that you are involved in the theft and smuggling of artefacts out of Egypt and I will be contacting the authorities dealing with this matter and I am sure they will want to speak to you at some length. I believe that you were using Titus to help you in this venture and in fact I think you would have used all of the members of this party to help you in one last haul before things became too bad.'

'PC Bailey, I merely organised the removal of rare and precious artefacts from the tombs of the great pharaohs to keep them safe from being plundered by the axis powers. Who knows what plans they would have for them if they fell into their hands?'

'I am not sure that the authorities see that you removing them and sending them back to England and then offering them to anyone who might be able to pay your price for them is as you put it 'keeping them safe' your Ladyship.'

'Well really Bailey this is too much. I shall make sure that Inspector Lansdowne hears of this!'

'I shall do likewise Lady Agatha'.

Lady Agatha adjusted her position in the chair so that she faced away from the Constable and was clearly going to have no further discussion in this matter with him.

'Now let me turn my attention to you Miss Mary-Belle Devine. You were very helpful to me earlier this evening when I had an unfortunate accident with a horse and cart. This act of kindness on your part and your general loveliness'

Faces turned in the room towards him

'I mean the fact that you appear so nice has thrown me off any thoughts that you could be the person who has carried out these crimes and yet when I look back over what has happened you have been right at the very scene of the crime on at least two occasions. You stood next to Monty when he took the drink and you were the one who called out that you had discovered the body of poor Titus. Now while I can't easily see how you could have doctored the drink for the Major, calling out that you had discovered the vicar would be a perfect cover for you to have been the person who killed him.'

Mary-Belle stood quietly next to Lady Agatha's chair. She clasped her purse in front of her with both hands which created the look of someone very demure. The pose was rehearsed and was obviously having the desired effect on the Policeman

'Surely PC Bailey you cannot believe that I am an agent of some kind and that I actually killed anyone!?'

'Oh but I do believe you have killed before Miss Devine.'

Mary-Belle dropped her purse and brought her hands to her face. Gasps once again echoed around the audience who were hanging on every word that the Constable uttered as if they were the closing remarks of the prosecution in the High Court.

'Oh yes Miss you may look shocked but I do believe you were involved in the death of your husband Dwight Devine. I do not believe you physically murdered him but I think you were well aware he had fallen overboard in his drunken stupor and you did nothing at all to help him, which resulted in him drowning with the body never being recovered but then the sharks probably put paid to that. Am I correct Miss Devine?'

Mary-Belle Devine slowly brought her hands away revealing the face of a broken woman.

'But he was a brute PC Bailey, on the surface he was a charming man but in private he was a monster. Yes, I heard the splash on deck and assumed he had fallen overboard and I was glad, glad do you hear me! But I will never admit I thought he was so drunk he couldn't swim back to the ladder and I will never admit that he called out for help because I didn't hear anything after that splash. For all I knew PC Bailey he might just have been taking a swim.

If you are asking me do I regret that he was lost, then the answer is no, a very definite no. But that doesn't mean I killed him and you may tell who you wish.'

She made to walk from the room but was halted by the servant PC Bailey had posted there just in case any one of the suspects felt they needed to get away.

'I will do just that Miss Devine and you must take your chances with them when you return to the United States which will be very shortly. But do I think you had anything to do with the murders that have taken place here this evening? You were friends with Monty and in fact I think you expected to find him here. From our conversation earlier I believe you and he had met a number of times after your first meeting at a polo match some years ago. You were accompanied at that meeting by your husband but I am not so sure your husband knew about any of the meetings afterwards. The two of you also met after his death and that is why there was an investigation into the Major's whereabouts at the time the incident happened but his alibi was very strong and so any accusations and rumours finished at that point.

All of this being true and the look on your face Miss Devine tells me it is, I believe you came here to continue your romance with the Major and that is why you wanted to speak to Titus alone. You knew you were late in booking your cabin and as he was in charge of that matter, you wanted to negotiate with him to ensure your cabin was either very close, perhaps even adjoining the Majors, or better still that you could secure a suite which would make any assignation you planned to be all the sweeter.

You had begun your conversation earlier with Titus when you discussed hat boxes but you were interrupted from getting around to cabin negotiations by Lady Agatha when she commanded Titus to say the Grace. Later on you saw your opportunity to continue your discussion with him privately when you noticed him leave the table. You assumed that he must be going back to his room for something and so you followed him. Is this correct Miss?'

'I did follow him up to his room for that very reason PC Bailey. I saw him leave and decided I didn't want to make it too obvious I was following him so I used one of the alternative stairs on my side of the room to get up to the first floor. I lost him and didn't know which room was his. I thought I could intercept him so went around the other side of the gallery but unfortunately there is a locked door in the far corner so I had to retrace my steps which delayed me somewhat.

By the time I arrived on the final remaining side of the gallery where his room must be, he had already disappeared so I called out. That was when I saw a light from under a door. I called out again and then knocked. I could hear some movement but no one answered so I tried the door handle and that's when I saw him lying there on the floor.'

She covered her face with her hands once more as she re-lived the scene of death she had seen earlier this evening. She began to sob. A woman arose from the nearest chair and offered it to her. Mary-Belle gladly accepted. The rapid rising and falling of the young woman's shoulders clearly showed the rest of the people assembled in the room how much the discovery of the body had affected her.

The sound of the hammer of a gun being cocked is unmistakable even if you have only ever heard it once in your life. In fact the sound is so unique, even if you have never heard it before, the thickly sounding 'click' as well-oiled metallic components snap securely into place tells the listener that here is something well made, something that has a purpose, something that should not be ignored.

'Enough of this painful drivel, I have stood here listening to your summing up Constable and frankly I am amazed that someone as bumbling and ineffective, as you clearly are, could possibly have deduced anything at all about what has gone on here.

I booked myself into the Pig & Whistle Inn, in the very heart of this dreary village three days ago and this morning I drove down to the station to take a look at the people arriving on the trains to see if I might be able to pick out Jennings, who I already knew was my contact, in the hope that I might have an opportunity to complete our business without the need to join this party at all. I had no luck there but I saw you Bailey getting off the Exeter train. I came over closer to you when you spoke to the station official and I overheard that you were making your way to Motley Hall. The last thing that I needed was a Policeman snooping about the place. Earlier on, I had noticed a hay cart waiting on the road to the Hall and saw an ideal opportunity to get you out of the way. So while you were still talking and sorting out your baggage I drove to the 'witches hat' cottage and on seeing there was nobody around I broke in and waited for you to pass by. You looked so foolish trying to balance those bags and were so preoccupied that you didn't notice me there in the window. After you passed by and turned up the lane, I got back into my car and quickly drove along the back road to the field and asked the young man who was working there for directions. When he was distracted, it was a simple task to overpower him and leave his body in the ditch. Then I took good aim with a blowpipe, that I have as part of my equipment, and a well-aimed dart sent that horse galloping off for all its worth in your direction. The lane would have been very narrow by the time the horse met you so I thought it was a certainty that you would be at the very least incapacitated but then when I saw you arrive later at the Hall looking like you had slept in a hay barn, I knew that my plan had failed. But on seeing how good you were at your job I thought I needn't have gone to all the trouble in the first place.

But maybe I was wrong not to have worried, you have managed to work your way through these two suspects and have arrived at an opinion that they could not be your murderer. So it is safe to assume that as I am the only other person standing here that you were about to come to me and to tell me why you believe that I am the person who has committed these murderous acts.

Now as much as I would find it mildly entertaining to listen to your thoughts on how and why, I have to leave very shortly so I will tell you myself.'

Edith Marrowbone stood facing her audience. Her black dress, now seeming to fit perfectly with her identity. In her right hand she held a Luger pistol levelled directly at PC Bailey. The servant made a small movement from the door and she quickly turned the gun on him.

'Don't be a fool man!' called Bailey.

'Listen to the Constable if you want to stay alive' Marrowbone's voice was low and sinister and the servant remained motionless pinned where he stood by the unwavering barrel of the gun that was trained on his heart.

'Now open the door and then move away, right away, over there by the good Constable where I can see you more easily. Quickly time is running out. Now Bailey, I need you to hand over that pile of photographs that you recovered from the vicar's bedroom. I see them there to your right, bring them over here and place them, very slowly, on this chair. Bailey did as he was instructed and returned to his place in the room directly opposite Marrowbone.

Marrowbone looked at the photographs for a moment noticing the ones still edged in blood, a macabre memento from her meeting with Titus Jennings.

'I know you won't believe this for a moment, any of you, but I deeply regretted having to kill the vicar.'

She paused and surveyed the room. The stony looks that met her gaze told her that she was correct in her assumption that not one person actually believed her.

'Thank you PC Bailey you have been most co-operative. I had you down as a fool but clearly even you know that when someone stands in front of you with a gun it is very good sense to do exactly what they ask you to do. But now I must be leaving. These troublesome photographs need to be delivered as soon as possible to the people who have paid me to obtain them. But before I leave let me put you all out of your misery and give you the reason why all of this happened in the first place.

I did it for the Fatherland, for Germany, I suppose you would term me a spy and yes that will do as a description. My mission was simple. I was to make contact and collect the photographs. Titus had been approached and had been recruited to our cause by our agents when he had been making one of his many visits to Casablanca on behalf of Lady Agatha as part of her smuggling operation which you, PC Bailey, have exposed.

Jennings was easy to recruit because although on the surface you may believe that his passion is the Church. Actually it is money or rather the lack of it in his case that really motivates him. We knew about his incident at the deanery in Stanton Drew and the fact that the offertory monies were never found in the safe following the fire, oh yes our research is thorough. So for a trifling sum really, Titus sold himself to us. Lady Agatha had arranged for him to take a flight over a very strategic base near the Nile Delta, she wanted to use the photographs as part of a book that she planned to work on in her retirement. We had a different use for those same photographs, and so the deal was set.

My plan was to meet up with Jennings two weeks ago but unfortunately I was delayed getting back into England which meant that I had to come here and join the party. It wasn't ideal with so many people around but worse still I discovered two things. Firstly, Lady Agatha was becoming very suspicious about Jennings' behaviour. I heard her talking earlier on the telephone that she wanted to leave a message for Inspector Lansdowne. She was explaining to whoever it was at the other end that she wanted Lansdowne to make further investigations into the mysterious fire at his previous employment where the money went missing. She finished the call abruptly as the person clearly wasn't getting the message properly and I heard her say that she would call Lansdowne early in the morning.

I put two and two together and realised that Lansdowne might think that the fire needed further investigation which could lead to Jennings not boarding the ship but instead being taken into custody for further questioning. I could not allow that to happen so I knew I had to complete the transaction as quickly as possible but given how difficult it might be to talk to Jennings this evening as he was so busy sorting out things for the trip, including establishing from which port we were to embark, I needed to make sure that her Ladyship didn't make that call in the morning. I noticed the way in which drinks were being ordered and then made my preparations. It was a simple enough task for someone with my training to wait for her to order a drink and then to momentarily distract the waiter and add something to her drink. Of course we all know what happened next which turned out to be a huge bonus because dear Monty turned out to be a spy. And that was my second discovery.

I could hardly believe my luck when Bailey read out the Major's mission letter. It made it clear that an advisor had joined the safari party. Well I knew that couldn't be me because my missions should have already been completed and also I have had no contact with my superiors for almost two weeks so no one could have known that I had joined the party.

This left only one possible answer and that was that a second agent had been deployed. This only happens when someone high up believes that either the first mission has failed or that the agent has become surplus to requirements. I knew that this agent would be looking to obtain the photographs and remove me from the scene at the same time but I had no idea who the agent was so I needed to be on my guard.

I found where Jennings was seated and joined him at the table but before I had a chance to discuss anything, he left to do Lady Agatha's bidding. So I slipped a note into his napkin and left the table. I watched from a distance to make sure he read the note. The idiot opened the napkin and he almost missed it completely but eventually I saw that he had read it. It clearly made him more agitated and before I had a chance to return to the table to give him the sign he jumped up and headed for the stairs. I realised in an instant that he was going back to collect the photographs from his room and so I followed him.

I mentioned earlier that it was money that motivated this man and it was money that was his eventual downfall because when I approached him in his room to make the exchange he refused saying that it had been more difficult to obtain the information than he had at first thought and wanted to be paid more. I didn't have time to negotiate and so I killed him. He was holding the photographs in his hand when I first entered the room and I had knocked him off balance causing him to drop them all over the floor but before I could retrieve them I heard Mary-Belle Devine calling his name in the corridor. I considered waiting for her and then kill her as well.'

A sharp intake of breath sang out across the room and Mary-Belle Devine held her hand to her mouth, a look of horror on her face once again.

'Oh yes Miss Devine'.

Marrowbone looked over at the terrified young woman.

'You have no idea how close you came to joining the vicar in the afterlife. However, I considered there might be too much noise so instead I made my exit through the second door but Miss Devine was now at the top of my list of suspects as being the second spy. But when I discovered that she had not taken the photographs when she raised the alarm I knew that it was not her I needed to worry about.

So that only left Lady Agatha who I was certain was not working for the Germans and Crispin Moorcock, the idiotic son of a Jewish merchant banker. Oh the irony of his cover, why had I not seen through it from the off!? Moorcock was clearly the agent and I knew that I would need to meet up with him and take my chances that I could in some way overpower him.

While Bailey was conducting his questioning of Miss Devine, I found myself seated close to Moorcock and took the opportunity to mention the codeword to him. We then met out in the corridor that led to the bathrooms. He was very well trained but perhaps he wasn't prepared for a woman with such determination, such passion.

And that is the point of all of this PC Bailey. I was never really interested in the money, it is passion that drives me, passion for the cause and passion for the one love of my life, my Rudi. He has taught me that you must stand up for what you believe in. It is the curse of this generation that too many of us accept our fate even though we are not happy with it and live out our life in a gloomy compromise awaiting our judgement day when we will be judged and it will all have been for nothing. Well that is not how I plan to live and there are many that are like minded. There is a new world coming. We will change the world.

I have indulged you all for far too long but it is important to me that you understand why these things are happening. There will be many terrible things very soon which will make you ask why. Hopefully you will think back to this moment and you will understand that it is the passion in your adversaries which make them unbeatable. We will prevail be assured of that.

Now I ask all of you to remain exactly where you are. I am sure I do not need to remind you that I will kill anyone who tries to stop me.'

Marrowbone edged towards the open door keeping the gun levelled on the occupants of the room. PC Bailey made no attempt to move he knew to do so would only put others in danger. He would wait for her to leave and then he would give chase.

'Once again Bailey you are the most incompetent Policeman I have ever had the pleasure of meeting, but if you are thinking of chasing me then I would suggest you start running….now!'

With that Marrowbone let off a shot into the air causing chaos inside the room. Bailey made for the door but people were dropping to the floor causing him to stumble once, twice and then he fell full length on to the floor winding him. He was up in a moment and running after Marrowbone up the small staircase and across the hallway where he first stood hours before taking in the splendour of the place, now Motley Hall looked different to him as he charged forwards, the front door was open and he burst out on to the steps. Marrowbone was ahead of him just about to run across the yard.

'Miss Marrowbone stay where you are you will never be able to escape on foot in that dress'

Edith Marrowbone stopped on hearing the voice of the Constable behind her. She was still carrying the gun and turned to aim it at Bailey. Just then lights came on to the left of Marrowbone, bright lights which were quickly accompanied by more to the side of them and then to the right and behind her until in seconds she was bathed in the bright headlights of vehicles on three sides. Marrowbone stood where she was but realising the futility of running any further she looked straight into the face of PC Bailey and brought the gun up to her own temple.

'Remember Bailey it was for passion.'

A single shot rang out and the lifeless body of Edith Marrowbone slumped on to the driveway.

Bailey ran over to her and as he did so he noticed shadows moving in front of the lights. He could hear the sounds of male voices half shouting but he didn't really take any notice of them. Instead he looked down at the figure lying in front of him. Her shot had caused a lot of damage to her head and Bailey now on his knees in the gravel had to look away. A firm hand grabbed his shoulder and an authoritative voice said 'It alright man, come away, you've done your bit. Let us take it from here'.

He looked up and turned towards the voice. The tall man was in plain clothes but he was flanked on either side by police officers so he assumed he was probably a detective.

'But where have you all come from, surely you haven't all been playing skittles have you?'

The man laughed. 'No Bailey we haven't. We have been waiting out here for you to flush them out and that is exactly what you did. Now let's get you back inside while we clear up here.

Bailey made his way back up the steps and into the hallway once more. There were people everywhere and many of them were policeman. He was having a hard time understanding where they had all come from. Things started to blur into one another and he finally realised that this had been a very long evening. He went off to his room and was told that Inspector Lansdowne would be here in the morning to put him fully in the picture.

Chapter Twenty One

PC Bailey was up bright and early and was eating a hearty breakfast just before eight o-clock, when a gentleman came over and joined him at the table.

'PC Bailey if I am not much mistaken. If I am, then I am not much of a detective after all. I'm Inspector Lansdowne of Scotland Yard'.

Bailey dropped his knife and fork with a start and stood to attention except that he had put his helmet on the next table and so couldn't reach it and in turn realised that he shouldn't salute but then still thought he ought to and so did in any case.

'No need Bailey. In fact if anyone should be saluting anyone it should be the other way around.'

'I, I don't follow Sir?'

'No well I can understand that but trust me on this one you were hand-picked for this role because we knew that your unique qualities would come to the fore in this very tricky case and they certainly did. Well done man!'

Bailey stared at the man in front of him. He was probably around thirty five years old and at least six foot two inches tall with a good complexion. He wore a good quality three piece pinstriped suit topped off with a dark blue trilby hat. He looked every inch a city gent rather than a police inspector but Bailey guessed that was how officers of his rank dressed when they worked at the 'Yard'. Lansdowne was looking at him and his big face and bright eyes were smiling. He looked genuinely pleased with Bailey.

'Oh, thank you Sir. I'm a bit bewildered if I am honest. I only came up here to do a bit of crowd control and then the murders started happening and I ended up with three of 'em getting killed, so I didn't expect to be standing here getting congratulated by an Inspector from Scotland Yard.'

'I think it's best if I put the whole thing in a nutshell for you and then I would like you to write up your reports here at Motley Hall. Once you have finished those and we have had a chance for a final chat my driver will take you back to the station in time for the four-thirty-eight to Exeter St David's, does that all sound all right with you Bailey?'

Bailey nodded.

'Excellent. Now first things first, let's get some more tea and a refresher on that breakfast and then we'll get started.'

Inspector Lansdowne attracted the attention of a hovering servant and effortlessly gave the food order before returning his attention to

Bailey. He placed his arms on the table and clasped his hands together in front of him.

'Now Bailey, where to begin? I think the first thing to tell you is that a lot of what you are going to here is not only confidential but is actually top secret and that's the reason why I need the report written here rather than at the station in Exeter. Do you understand?'

Bailey nodded again.

'Good man, well the fact is Bailey we received information some time ago that a spy would be joining this safari party. We didn't have any idea who it might be, not even if it was a male or a female. We also knew that the Major worked for the secret service and would be joining the party in an attempt to discover who the spy was from the inside as it were.

Where you fitted in was that we needed to have a police presence but we didn't want anyone who would be too officious and perhaps upset the apple cart. We needed someone who would be there but wouldn't be there if you see what I mean?'

'Er no, not exactly Sir because I was definitely there.'

'Yes I know that Bailey, you're not really following this but anyway let's press on because there is a lot to get through.'

'Right ho Sir, so I'm there, or here, I suppose I should say, but at the same time not really. I've got that now Sir.'

'Splendid, you see it's the way you catch on to this sort of thing that made you invaluable in the success of this operation. Having you doing crowd control for my dear friend Lady Agatha allowed us to have police on the ground but just a light touch. Obviously as it turned out the touch may have been a little too light as we ended up with three victims inside and the murderess dead on the driveway. However there is nothing for you to worry about Bailey, you did your job as well as anyone expected you to and in the end the photographs didn't fall into the hands of the Germans so that is all to the good.

Now I would like you to get started on those reports because we don't want to delay you getting home do we?'

With that Inspector Lansdowne stood up and signalled to a junior detective to come over and then turned back to Bailey.

'This is Detective Sergeant Tom Roberts. When you are finished here he will show you through to the study where he will be able to assist you with the report. Thank you again Bailey for all your good work here. No one can imagine what might have happened if those photos had fallen into the wrong hands, it makes me shudder just to think about it.'

Inspector Lansdowne shook Bailey's hand and then left the room.

Bailey made one last circuit with a piece of bread around his plate and pushed it away from him. Detective Roberts watched him from across the table.

'I'm ready now Sir'

Roberts led the way to the study and indicated to a chair in front of a small table on which was set a typewriter. To the right hand side was a pile of plain paper and carbons.

Bailey set to work. There was a lot to type up and on more than one occasion Roberts ordered in mugs of tea. They took a half an hour break for lunch and then eventually as the early afternoon sun began to make its way around to the study windows a pile of (fairly neat) paper lay to the left of the table. Detective Roberts read through them slowly making small corrections with his stubby note pencil. From time to time his eyebrows raised and he looked up from the paper and shook his head slowly in the direction of Bailey. Finally, he shuffled the papers together, stood up and left the room. Bailey looked around, this was the room where he had brought the body of Monty and laid him on this very desk after he had drunk the poison that was intended for Lady Agatha.

Inspector Lansdowne came in behind him.

'Ah Bailey, finished at last. As I mentioned at breakfast I would pop in to see you before you left. Detective Roberts has already taken your bags out to my car. I know this has all been a bit of an occasion one way and another. Tricky to take in and all that but trust me Bailey you have done a first rate job and I can't thank you enough. I will make sure that your superiors including your desk sergeant hear all about it'.

Oh dear, thought Bailey. I had forgotten about him. He gave me strict instructions not to muck it up this time. I suppose if Inspector Lansdowne is going to say that I did well, perhaps he will overlook just the three little deaths and the fact that one of them a secret agent an all!

He made his way out to the waiting car. Roberts stood with the rear door already open for him.

Bailey nodded and removed his helmet ready to get in when he heard the bright tones of a car horn close by. He looked around and saw a very distinctive sports car with an equally distinctive woman in the driving seat. She wore a bright yellow dress and headscarf to match, as he walked over to the car Mary-Belle broke into a huge smile, she looked like summer herself he thought.

'Well PC Bailey, there were times in your investigation when I really wondered if you were ever going to solve anything at all and yet at the end of the day you came up trumps as you English like to say. You must be very proud. I understand that the rather dashing Inspector Lansdowne thinks so too. I am aware that you think I murdered my husband but I really didn't you know.

There is a possibility that I mistook the splash for a large fish, perhaps it was a shark' she chuckled to herself, the irony of what she had said not being lost on her at all but completely lost on Bailey as usual 'Or I suppose it may have been the sound of my dear drunken brute of a husband falling over the side and yes on the face of it perhaps I should have gone up on deck much earlier than I did just to make sure that that pig of man was actually all right.

But the fact remains that I didn't, and there isn't a court in this land, or anywhere else that won't believe me. So whatever you may think I will not be going to jail.'

She signalled for Bailey to lean forward and she kissed him full on the cheek leaving a bright red mark that matched the colour his face was rapidly turning.

'You know PC Bailey if you were not already married I would really want to see you again!'

With that she gunned the engine and Bailey stepped away from the sports car as it turned and moved off at speed along the drive churning up dust from the gravel that only the night before had been stained with the blood from Edith Marrowbone when she finally realised that there really was for her no alternative, no escape. Her last words still rang in his ears 'for passion Bailey, for passion'.

He returned to Lansdowne's car and sank down into the sumptuous seat and drank in the smell of the leather upholstery. This really was a magnificent motor car. Roberts closed the door and the driver moved the car effortlessly away down the drive turning right at the gates and back along the lane where Bailey had met the horse and cart and almost met his maker the evening before.

At the station, the driver helped him out with his bags and then bid him farewell and with an expertly executed three-point turn disappeared back along the lane towards the hall.

Bailey stood for a moment watching the elegant motor car thinking how much he would like to own one of them when his thoughts were interrupted by a familiar voice.

'I have to say I am disappointed in you, PC Bailey!'

Bailey turned to be confronted by the Midloxton Under Stationmaster with a very stern look on his face. Even his moustache looked stern.

'Ah Jones'

'That's Johnson Sir'

'Yes Johnson. What appears to be the problem?'

'Well sir I am sure that you will recall that because of circumstances beyond my control I afforded you the use of a sack truck to make your journey easier up to Motley Hall.'

'Yes indeed Johnson, I do and it did make the journey far better. I must tell you that your idea of a mile and a half is a bit different to mine and without that truck, my arms would have been around my ankles by the time I would have arrived at the crossroads, let alone the Hall.'

'Well where is it?'

'You know perfectly well where it is, it's along this lane and then turn at the crossroads...'

'Not the Hall, of course I know where that is. I mean the sack truck!'

'Oh I see. Oh, now that's a problem. You see I have left it at the Hall. Well at least I think that's where it will be. I had a bit of a problem on the way involving a horse and cart but the truck survived very well apart from the sticky wheel, but it had that when you gave it to me.'

'So I will now need to go up to the Hall to retrieve it I suppose? This is most irregular and is definitely not covered in the GWR Regulations Handbook!'

'I am sorry about that but there were also other incidents up at the Hall which distracted me. I am sure I can arrange for one of the servants or one of the Police cars to return it to you.'

'Most irregular, really most irregular I will have to fill in a report!'

With that Johnson turned and walked through the gate back into the station. PC Bailey followed him and as hardly anyone was waiting for the train he took the opportunity of sitting on one of the benches that lined the platform.

He placed his suitcase by his side at the end of the bench and his small bag on the top. He noticed that the case had a number of deep scratches along one side and that one corner was slightly dented in; all the result of the horse and cart he thought to himself....lucky the suitcase didn't end up in the stream come to think of it.

As he sat there in the afternoon sunshine, his thoughts drifted to the conversation he knew he would be having with his desk sergeant later tomorrow morning when he arrived back at Heavitree Police Station in Exeter. He couldn't say he was looking forward to it.

All at once there was a shrill whistle heralding the London train as it steamed into Midloxton station. The bright green engine shrouded in clouds of steam with plumes of grey smoke billowing from its stack. Bailey was always impressed by trains; they had fascinated him all his life even as a small boy and he had spent many hours with his mother watching them arrive and leave Exeter St David's station.

He opened the carriage door and boarded the train closing it behind him. He placed his luggage in the carriage and returned to look out of the door once more. Johnson arrived still looking perturbed about his missing sack truck.

'Good day to you PC Bailey. I trust you will write in your report the help that Great Western Railways provided to the Police in this matter, notwithstanding the missing sack truck, we are of course very happy to have been of service.'

'Indeed I will and thank you once again.'

Johnson looked to the guard and nodded. He in turn gave a whistle and signalled the train was clear to leave. The driver returned the whistle and the train jolted forwards and onwards. Midloxton was soon lost in clouds of steam.

Bailey closed the window and returned to his carriage.

There were only two other passengers in the carriage, an elderly woman with a tiny black hat perched right on the top of her head. The lady had produced some sort of sewing from her bag which was between her feet. From time to time she leant forward and selected something from the bag. Each time Bailey expected the hat to fall on the floor but it was so tightly pinned to her hair that it remained fast, much to Bailey's fascination.

Bailey took the seat opposite the woman and watched her for a while as the countryside flashed by the window.

'Excuse me madam, do you make many train journeys?'

The woman looked up and nodded 'oh yes I make this journey quite often. I have a friend who I visit in Exeter'

'Well then this may be something that you have never considered but don't you think it's amazing that when we go into the tunnels, we can still see each other because the lights turn on!'

'Oh God, I don't believe it!!!!' was the utterance from of the gentleman passenger in the carriage who had been engrossed in his newspaper, which now remained solidly in place.

The old woman looked first in the direction of the gentleman who appeared now to be quietly sobbing, and then she looked at Bailey who beamed back at her. She looked puzzled firstly at why the gentleman should make such a reaction to the comment and then at the policeman

133

as to how with thoughts like that, how did he ever make it into the police force!?

PC Bailey will return in......

'Who killed Santa Claus?'

Printed in Great Britain
by Amazon